The
Third Law

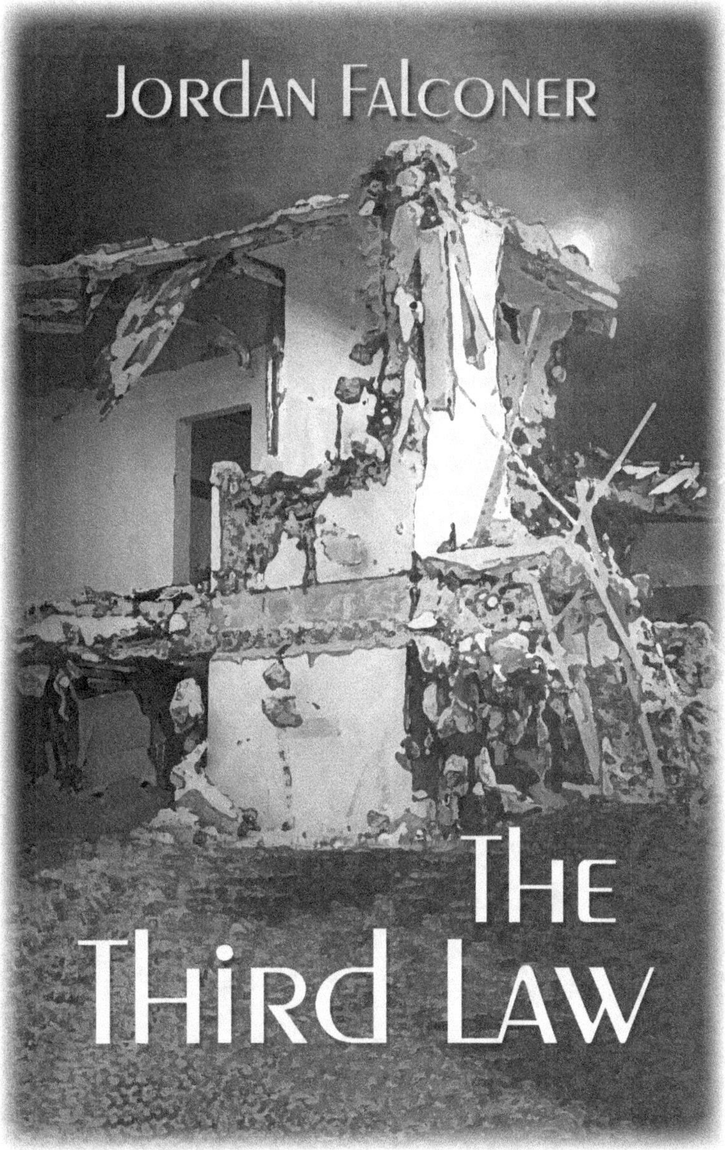

Jordan Falconer

The Third Law

Mindancer Press
Bedazzled Ink Publishing Company * Fairfield, California

978-1-943837-32-8 paperback

Cover design
by
C.A. Casey

Mindancer Press
a division of
Bedazzled Ink Publishing Company
Fairfield, California
http://mindancerpress.bedazzledink.com

For Tammy who never lets me give up

Thank you to Casey and Claudia for
making me sound better than I really am

Foreword

I admit it.

I nearly *died* when Claudia and Casey asked me to write a book about my immigration experiences. I tried to gracefully say no but that wasn't really an option.

I have never wanted to do anything less in my entire life. I still don't want to *think* about it, much less write about it. I *loathe* talking about it.

I don't want to whine. I'm not looking for sympathy or condolences. At the same time, I don't want you to think that it's damaged me in some fundamental way. It hasn't. It's just . . . *over* . . . you know? It's past. It's faded into nightmare, as it should.

I don't like to talk about it directly, so I was really glad when they mentioned to me that it was okay for it to be a work of fiction and to do it any way I wanted.

I did so. This is the result.

My personal immigration experience was a soul sucking, mind destroying ordeal of misery that last ten long years. Although you won't find skirmishes with any country's border patrol, or mountains of paperwork, you *will* find how horrible it felt on the inside. You'll see how it felt to be thought of as a degenerate. How you can be an outsider in your own home. How you're somehow *less* than other human beings simply because of your sexual orientation. You'll find out what it's like to feel insecure and clingy, to wake up in the night, sweating in terror.

That being said, I'm hoping you enjoy the ride.

And yes, there *is* a light at the end of the tunnel - and it's *not* the headlight of an oncoming train. Things always work out the way they should, even if it doesn't feel like that when you're going through them.

Peace,
~~~ Jordan ~~~

Newton's Third Law
For every action there is an equal and opposite reaction

CHAPTER 1

"IT'S DOWN HERE," a tall, gangly man said, gesturing before him into the darkness.

Glen Adams nodded. "Okay, I'll get started."

"Can I get you anything? Coffee? Water?" Victor Hadley gave Glen another inane smile.

Glen smiled at him, trying to suppress his dislike. "Just some water, please."

Victor's grin increased. "All right. I'll just show you the server, and then I'll be off." He turned and walked down a darkened path between the widely spaced racks of servers. The fluorescent lights flickered on overhead with a buzzing sound that was barely audible over the noise of the industrial air conditioning. The air smelt faintly of ozone.

They walked in pools of light to almost the middle of the cavernous room. As they left an area, the lights flickered out and a new set over and just ahead of them flickered on. The blinking lights of power supplies and hard drives reflected off the glass doors covering the server racks.

Glen glanced around the room. It was cold and he felt even colder in the overhead air conditioning.

"Bit creepy, isn't it?" Victor said with a half-smile. He opened the door to a rack, and pulled out a keyboard and mouse

Glen almost unwillingly nodded.

"The room was designed for much larger equipment. PABXs got a lot smaller after this room was built." Victor shrugged. "It doesn't help that this room is underground."

"Well, this is the Department of Defense." Glen shrugged.

"True." Victor straightened. "Okay, I'll back in a jiffy. Water, right?"

Glen nodded. "Yep. Water."

Victor gave him a sharp nod and walked off.

Glen watched him go. *What a dork.*

Pools of light flickered on and off in the distance, marking Victor's departure from the computer room.

Glen leaned forward and stared at the computer screen. *Crap, it's locked. He never gave me the password. Now I'm going to have to wait for him to get back.*

Glen looked around into the darkness. *This place really* is *huge.* He watched fractured reflections of himself and ghostly lights in the smoky doors stretching off into the distance in front and to the sides of him. The lights flickered off above him, startling him.

Of course. They're on a sensor. Glen quickly took a few steps along the aisle and the lights flickered on again. He loosened his tie. *This is going to be a long day.* He glanced at his watch. *Just after nine thirty. This is going to be one* long *fucking installation.*

He pulled out his cell phone. *No signal,* it said. He shrugged. That sounded about right—he was underground, virtually entombed in concrete. *I hope they have a landline in here.*

In the distance, he heard the ding of the elevator. *Great. Victor's already back.*

He waited for the pools of light that would signal Victor's return.

The room remained dark.

Glen frowned. *That's really weird.*

He headed back the way they'd come, bathed in fluorescent light. He got to the door and hesitated. *If I leave, I'm not going to be able to get back in again.* He shrugged and craned his neck. He peered into the distance, trying to make out the elevator doors through the glass. They were distorted and seemed to be closed.

Wierd. When the doors ding like that it means they're open or opening.

He backed up slightly with a sigh and glanced at his watch again. Nine thirty five.

Bored, he glanced through the glass down the other side of the corridor. He saw a down arrow in the darkness, about three quarters of the way up the wall.

Another *lift? I don't remember seeing that when we got down here.* He opened the door, and it began to beep. *Alarmed. Can't hold it open for long.*

He stuck his head out into the corridor. He glanced left and right. To the right was the lift he'd come down and to the left, another lift. This one was much darker and utilitarian. He could barely make it out in the darkness.

Wonder what's below us?

He grinned. It was probably a question Victor couldn't answer and therefore appealed to Glen to ask. He could imagine Victor's response.

The beeping on the door began to speed up and Glen hurriedly took a step back and closed it. *I don't want a bunch of security guards around me when it goes off.*

He turned and began to head back to the server he was supposed to be working on.

The door beeped and there was a sharp click as it unlocked.

Glen grinned. "Oh, good. You're back. You forgot—" He turned and saw that he was still alone. He frowned as the door clicked shut. "Victor?"

The silence stretched out, punctuated by the hiss of the air conditioning.

"What the hell?" Glen muttered. He took a step back the way he'd come. "Victor?" he called, a little louder.

He thought he heard footsteps ahead and to the right of him.

A pool of light flickered into being.

"Not funny, Victor," he said, walking toward it. The lights flickered off and footsteps, this time much louder, moved away from him. The light marked their path.

That can't be Victor. It would be completely unprofessional to try to scare the crap out of me. It's pretty fucking juvenile, actually. So who the hell is down here with me?

The lights flickered off in the distance, while he remained bathed in a comforting pool of harsh, white light.

They must be standing still. Who the hell is that?

He made his way toward where he'd last seen the light.

Two aisles up. He hurried toward another pool of light that flickered down the next aisle.

His palms began to sweat.

He quickly rounded the closest server rack, intent on startling the other person in the computer room.

The elevator dinged in the distance. A couple of seconds later the computer room door beeped and clicked open.

"Hey, Glen," Victor said, striding through the door and holding a bottle of water.

Suddenly the air shimmered and Victor's voice deepened.

"I totally forgot to give you the password to the server," Victor slurred. He moved in slow motion as shimmering waves of flashing light washed over them. Glen felt foggy and encased in molasses.

The queasy sensation continued on for several seconds and the flashes of light became blinding.

The light abruptly ceased.

"What the hell was that?" Glen asked as soon as he could speak again. He accepted the bottle of water Victor thrust at him, and took a swig.

"What?" Victor asked, looking curiously at him.

"The lights?"

Victor gave him a neutral stare. "What lights?"

"You can't tell me you didn't notice that. The flashing lights. You sounded like you were a broken record."

Victor gave him a neutral stare. "No, Glen. I didn't see anything."

Glen searched his face for signs of deception. *How the hell could he not notice what just happened?* Victor looked just as annoyingly guileless as he had when they'd first introduced themselves. "Nothing, I guess."

"Glen, are you feeling all right?"

Glen nodded. "I'm fine." Feeling uneasy, he led the way back to the server. "I wanted to ask you. Where does the other lift go to?"

"What other lift?" Victor asked.

"The one down the other end of the corridor?" Glen asked.

"Glen, there's only one lift to this level. It's the one you and I came down."

"All right, so you can't tell me. It's top secret or something."

Victor pulled him to a halt. "No, Glen," he said, slowly and clearly. "There's no lift down here except for the one you and I came down."

"I saw it at the end of the corridor. Look, if you can't tell me, that's fine. I know perfectly well DoD stuff isn't my business."

Victor eyed him for a moment. "Come with me." He turned and Glen shrugged.

Victor opened the door and gestured for Glen to lead.

"Show me this magical lift," Victor said.

Glen's temper sparked and he turned down the corridor to the left. The lights obediently flickered to life ahead of him. He frowned as he came to a stop before a concrete wall.

"It was right here." He glanced at Victor. He patted the wall, unable to resist. He half expected to feel smooth metal beneath his fingertips. There was nothing but cold concrete. "It was *here*, I tell you." He stared at Victor. "I *swear* it was here." He felt icy cold and his heart began to hammer. "What the hell is going on?"

Victor shrugged. "Nothing's going on here, Glen. There's only one lift. Why did you think there were two?"

"I heard the damn thing, that's why."

"Glen, calm down. Maybe you just heard one of the servers or alarm or something. It *is* a bit creepy down here." Victor gestured toward the glass marking the border of the computer room.

"Creepy be damned. This place is just weird."

Victor snorted a laugh. "Yeah, the tiny country town and subterranean computer room will play on your nerves after a while."

Glen frowned at him. He felt his hackles rise. He pushed his temper down and forced a grin. "Yeah. I guess so."

"Okay, you want to get started so you can get out of the Twilight Zone?" Victor asked.

Glen glanced sharply at him.

Victor's eyes flickered.

"Okay." Glen felt on edge and wanted nothing more than to be done with the entire, miserable trip.

Victor nodded and led him back into the computer room.

They stood in front of the server.

Victor rapidly tapped some keys on the keyboard. "That's the password. Got it?"

Glen nodded. "I think so."

"Good." Victor glanced at his watch. "I have a meeting now and I'll be back in half an hour. Are you going to be okay for that long?"

Glen nodded. "Yeah, I'll be fine." *I hope. This place is way fucking creepy.*

"Good." Victor turned away. "I'll be back in half an hour. If you need anything, there's a phone right next to the door. Dial zero and you'll get reception. They can ping me if you need me."

He was gone before Glen had a chance to respond.

Glen fished in his briefcase for a CD. *I just want to get this done and get the hell out of here.*

He saw rainbows and stared at his hands. The air shimmered and flickered uneasily, as though he were under water. Contrails of color bled out of the end of his fingertips and lightning flashed before his eyes. He collapsed to his knees, suddenly weak. The light gained in intensity and he closed his eyes against the glare. He curled up, feeling waves of static electricity prickling his skin uncomfortably. He held his eyes tightly closed as light drilled into them. He moaned in pain.

Holy mother of god, what the fuck is going on here?

The light and prickling sensation subsided. He painfully pulled himself to his knees. He was soaked in sweat and his heart hammered in his chest. A wave of nausea passed over him and he clutched his stomach, uncertain that the water he'd drunk would stay down. After a few terrible seconds, the sensation passed.

Glen slowly and painfully levered himself to his feet, clutching his aching and throbbing head.

Oh, crap. I'm sick. I have to get out of here.

Breath swept in and out of his lungs like sandpaper. His eyes throbbed and watered.

He heard a beep in the distance and a click as the computer room door opened. He headed toward the sound, intent on calling Victor and leaving.

Kelly and Rowan are going to kill me.

He limped toward the door, barely aware of the pool of light that slid away to one side of him.

He reached the door and blinked uncertainly at the telephone perched on the wall beside it. There was no keypad.

How the hell am I meant to dial zero? For god's sake he's such a dick.

He heard a soft footstep behind him. He felt a surge of relief. Footsteps meant people and a means of escape.

"Look," he said, turning around. "I need . . ." His mind went blank and he forgot what he was going to say.

There, in front of him, stood a duplicate of himself.

Almost the same, he corrected himself after a second or so of pure shock. His eyes weren't as hard and he wasn't as muscular. His hair was longer than the buzz cut his doppelganger had, and he wasn't wearing stained fatigues. The other version of him looked like a soldier and Glen wasn't one of those.

"What the fuck?" he asked. His soft words broke his doppelganger's apparent paralysis.

The other man snarled and lunged toward Glen.

Glen was unceremoniously dumped onto his back, the man on top of him.

The man was incredibly strong. Glen, feeling weak and disoriented, was unable to hold him off. He was dimly aware of a large hunting knife arcing toward his chest.

Suddenly the man's arm slowed and light began to bleed from it. Glen watched with almost clinical interest as his distorted face slowly creased into a jagged mask of fury. Glen felt dismay as the light flashed and his limbs felt encased in concrete. The man gave a wordless cry of rage, a deep roar, and forced the knife toward Glen's chest.

Light flashed before Glen's eyes and a soundless humming filled his ears. He felt as though his teeth were trying to vibrate out of his head. Then the pain came, exquisite and all consuming, as the knife plunged deep into his chest.

He screamed.

There was one, final, gargantuan blast of pure, white light and Glen knew no more.

CHAPTER 2

"I DON'T KNOW what kind of show you think you're running down there, but this is unacceptable."

Rowan May, Director of Technical Support Services for Octahedron Software, stared at her desk phone as though it'd turned into a snake.

"I apologize," she said smoothly. "I'm not up to speed with your issue. Could you please tell me what the problem is?"

That seemed to upset the man on the other end of the phone. "That's what I thought. Completely unprofessional. Do any of you have any clue what you're doing?"

"Again, Mr. Crossland, I'd like to help you but you have to tell me what's happened."

"Glen Adams is what's happened," Crossland snarled. "He's unprofessional and completely incompetent."

Rowan's eyebrows shot skyward. "*Glen?*"

"Yes. Glen Adams. He comes up here, starts acting like a madman, insults my network manager, runs out of the building, and hasn't been back. You're supposed to be the market leader for monitoring software. What kind of joke is this? I expect someone to be at site tomorrow or we're not paying for any of this and we're withdrawing from the contract. Your stockholders aren't going to like any of that once it becomes public knowledge, and it will. *Quickly.*"

Oh, hell. David's going to be very *pissed*. Rowan brought up an instant messaging session and eyed her list of contacts. Kelly Carne, her Technical Support Manager, showed as available. She gave brief grin.

Kelly, you have a minute? I need to see you in my office right now, she typed.

"I don't know what's happened," Rowan said. "But I'll

personally take care of this. My support manager and I will be up there tomorrow."

On my way, Kelly replied.

Crossland was silent a moment. "You'd better be. We paid good money for your solution and we want it in and running before the end of the week."

Rowan glanced at her calendar. Tuesday. If they flew up in the evening, they could stay in Rockhampton overnight and begin the five hour drive to Settler's Creek early in the morning. They could be there by nine. If she did the training and Kelly did the installation they'd be able to make Friday end of day. Barely.

"We can be there for a ten o'clock start tomorrow morning," she said.

"See that you are," Crossland said, sounding slightly mollified.

There was a click as the line disconnected.

Rowan stared at the receiver. She felt waves of unreality crashing over her. She tried to sift through the strange conversation she'd just had. Glen Adams had never gotten anything other than stellar reviews from all of their customers. He was calm, steady, levelheaded, and self-sufficient. She wondered what had happened to him.

"What's up?" Kelly Carne leaned comfortably in the doorway.

Rowan eyed her appreciatively. She felt her heart flip flop. Her elegant support manager wore a clinging business suit and a small grin creased her beautiful features. Her dark hair cascaded down her back and her dark eyes lit up with pleasure at the sight of her boss.

"Come on in," Rowan said.

Kelly sauntered into the room and sank down into the visitor's chair on the other side of Rowan's desk. Her gaze swept Rowan from top to bottom, skipping away from her breasts as though burned.

"You and I are going to be in Settler's Creek tomorrow morning," Rowan said.

Kelly's mouth dropped open. "Glen's already up there. What do they need to see us for? What's happened?"

"Just a sec." Rowan opened another instant messaging session.

Barb, she typed. *Can you get Kelly and I up to Rockhampton tonight? We have to be in Settler's Creek for a ten o'clock start tomorrow morning. We can fly back Saturday afternoon.*

Let me see what I can do, was Barb Mitchell's response a moment later.

"Sorry, Kell." Rowan looked up. She leaned back in her chair. "Have you heard from Glen?"

Kelly shook her head. "Nope. I wasn't expecting to hear from him until today some time. Installation should be over this afternoon and he should be starting training tomorrow."

"Huh," Rowan said. "I just got off the phone with a very angry Ryan Crossland. From DoD in Settler's Creek. Apparently Glen was rude, nasty, and incompetent. And he didn't show up to site today."

Kelly stared at her. "*Glen?* Are you *kidding* me?"

"No." Rowan sighed. "This deal is a lot of money for us. We have to go up and give Octahedron Software a good plug until the end of the week. If we don't, this is going to blow up worse than it already has." She smiled, despite her unease. "Hope you don't have any plans for the week."

"Just a hot date tonight, which I'm going to have to cancel."

"Ugh. You can always blame me." Rowan winced and shoved down a surge of jealousy. "Sorry, Kell, but I can't leave you behind. You're coming with me. You think you can handle the install?"

Kelly nodded. "Of course I can."

"Good. I don't know how far he got."

"Even if he dropped the ball—and I'm still having trouble believing that—I can do it in a day. Easy."

Rowan's e-mail dinged. It was a new message from Barb Mitchell. She opened it and scanned the attachments. She grinned at Kelly. "We have a three p.m. flight this afternoon to Rockhampton. We grab our car and head to our motel. We get something approaching a good night's sleep and drive to Settler's Creek in the morning."

"When do we hit Rockie?" Kelly asked with a sigh.

"About seven. We have an hour-and-a-half layover in Brisbane. We'll leave here around lunch, pack, and head north."

Kelly nodded. She looked concerned. "What exactly did they tell you about Glen?"

"All he said was pretty much what I told you. Are you sure he didn't call anyone? Rich Brennan maybe?"

"I'll ask Rich," Kelly said. "As far as I know, though, no."

"Has this ever happened before?"

Kelly looked sharply at her. "No *of course* not. You know Glen. He's just not like that."

"That's what I thought," Rowan said. *Morning, Rich*, she typed. *Can I see you a minute?*

Sure thing, boss, was Rich's response.

"I just asked Rich to join us," Rowan said in response to Kelly's questioning glance.

"Yeah, this isn't going to be pretty," Kelly said.

Rich's six-foot-six frame filled the doorway. "You called, boss?"

"Take a seat and close the door behind you," Rowan said.

Rich did as he was told. He glanced between the two of them.

"Have you heard from Glen in the last couple of days?" Kelly asked.

Rich shook his head. "No. Should I have?"

Rowan and Kelly exchanged a glance. Rich looked between them.

"Is there something wrong?" he asked.

"He wasn't himself at site yesterday," Kelly said.

Rowan snorted. "That's one way to put it."

"What did he do?" Rich asked.

"He took off from site and no one's seen him since he left," Kelly said.

"*What?*" Rich said. "*Glen?*"

"Yes. Glen."

"Then don't you think you should be calling the police or something?" Rich asked.

"He's not missing yet," Rowan said. "For all we know he's

holed up in his hotel. Or he's headed back here. Do either of you have his cell phone number? I don't know it off the top of my head."

"Can I have the phone?" Rich asked.

Rowan nodded and pushed it toward him. He hit the speaker phone button and quickly dialed Glen's number. Much to Rowan's surprise, Glen answered after two rings.

"Hello?" Glen asked hesitantly.

Rowan frowned. *That doesn't sound like him at all.*

"Hi, Glen," Kelly said.

"Who is this?" Glen asked after a moment of crackly silence.

All three exchanged a glance.

"Kelly."

Silence.

"Your boss."

Silence.

Kelly's eyes widened. "Glen? Not even kind of funny."

"Glen?" Rich asked.

The line went dead.

"What the hell was that?" Kelly asked.

Rich quickly stabbed the keypad again. This time the phone rang out and went to voicemail.

"Well," Rowan said. "At least we know he's safe."

"Maybe," Kelly said. "But I think he's lost his marbles."

"Too many trees?" Rich asked helpfully.

Rowan and Kelly gave him neutral stares.

He held up his hands. "Look, he's in the middle of nowhere. I never heard from him today and I was kind of surprised not to. I was at least expecting him to check in with me. I was supposed to be backing him up if anything went south. I'm just glad he's not kidnapped, dead, or gone walkabout."

"He may as well have," Rowan said. "He's in a world of hurt when I catch up to him."

"I don't know that I'd take that approach with him," Kelly said. "He didn't sound right on the phone. I hope he stays put until we get up there."

"He wouldn't bail," Rich said. "He's too much of a professional for that."

"So we all keep saying. The problem is, he isn't showing that part of his personality right now. In fact, he's making us look bad," Rowan said, silencing them both. "Kell, meet me at the airport at two."

"Sure," Kelly said with an easy grin.

She took that as her signal to leave and left, Rich close behind her. Rowan stared after them.

She shook her head. *Time to face the music with David.* She sighed and opened another instant messaging session.

Good morning, David, she typed. *You have a minute for your favorite director?*

It took a moment for David to respond. *LOL Sure thing, Rowan. Come on in.*

ROWAN PULLED UP into her driveway with a sigh and glanced at her watch. Just after twelve thirty. *Cool. Plenty of time to pack and head to the airport.*

She got out of her company car just as her phone rang.

She glanced at the number. Kelly.

"Hey, Kell," she said, smiling.

"Hey, Rowan," Kelly said.

"What can I do for you?"

"Could you please give me a lift to the airport?"

"Sure. No problem. What's your address?" She rifled in her laptop bag. "Hold on a sec, I just have to grab a pen and some paper."

"You ready?" Kelly asked after a minute.

"Shoot," Rowan said.

Kelly gave her the address.

"Rosebery, isn't that right on top of the airport?" Rowan asked.

"Yep, hence the request for a lift," Kelly said. "It's murder trying to get a taxi. No one wants the short fare."

Rowan grinned. "No problem. Is there going to be space for me to pull up on Gardeners Road?"

"Probably not. There's an alleyway at the back that runs parallel to it. Just come down there. All the way to the dead end."

"No problem," Rowan said. "I'll see you in what? Forty five minutes?"

"Sounds good to me."

"Okay. I'll see you in a bit."

"No worries, Rowan."

Rowan hung up with a smile and let herself into her house. *We live close to each other. Easy to get to.* The pleasant tingle she always got when she spoke to Kelly evaporated as the memory of her conversation with David filtered back into her mind.

He'd clearly been angry. *You could barely call that a conversation. Fix it and fix Glen. Or else. The* or else *part means I'd end up looking for another job if this goes south. We* all *will.*

Rowan's house was warm and still and she quickly changed into jeans and a tee shirt, and packed for three days. *On the bright side, at least I get to spend three days with Kelly. She's such a sweetie.*

Rowan quickly locked her house and drove to Rosebery. It didn't take her long and she arrived there at five to two. Kelly was waiting out the back for her. She looked dejected.

"Hey," Rowan said, leaning out of her window. "What gives?"

"I'm in trouble," Kelly said glumly as she tossed her luggage onto the back seat and climbed into the car. "My hot date was super pissed. I think it's going to be over when I get back."

Rowan winced, glancing over her shoulder as she turned around in the narrow alleyway. "What an idiot."

"*She's* an idiot."

"Okay, *she's* an idiot."

Kelly was silent for a moment. "Me being into girls isn't going to be a problem for you, is it?"

"Nope," Rowan said smoothly. She almost laughed. *Oh, hell no.*

They were comfortably silent for a few moments as Rowan navigated the short drive to the airport.

"What did David say?" Kelly asked.

Rowan pulled into a parking spot. "He didn't say much and he wasn't pleased."

Kelly winced. "This is going to be a *long* trip. When I get my hands on Glen, he's in serious shit."

"What do you think has happened to him? You know him better than I do."

"I have no clue," Kelly said slowly. "He's absolutely nothing like what either Ryan Crossland said or what he sounded like on the phone. He's steady, strong, and confident. Clients love him because he makes them feel comfortable. He's very smart and can think his way out of almost every nasty situation he finds himself in. He gets on like a house on fire with Rich and between them there's absolutely *no* technical situation my department can't handle." She pulled Rowan to a halt and studied her carefully. "I have a really bad feeling about this."

"I agree. This doesn't feel right. *Nothing* about this feels right." Rowan pulled Kelly into motion and they went into the airport terminal.

CHAPTER 3

"CAN I BUY you two ladies a drink?"

Rowan looked up at the man leaning toward them and smiling. He was in a rumpled, dark business suit. He wore a wedding ring. He was trying to surreptitiously eye her from top to bottom and not stare at her breasts.

Creep.

She glanced at Kelly. She looked annoyed.

"I'm sorry." Rowan finished off her coffee. "Can't. We're headed to our connecting flight."

"Thanks, though." Kelly stood and grabbed her leather jacket.

Rowan quickly walked out of the bar and headed toward their departure gate. It was almost four. She glanced at Kelly. She still looked angry.

Kelly caught her eye. "Fucking idiot. He was married and everything."

Rowan grinned. "There's always one, isn't there?"

Suddenly Kelly's eyes widened. "What the fuck?"

"Huh?"

Kelly swiveled around, and Rowan turned a second behind her, in time to see a man in jeans and a tee shirt running away from them and down a bank of escalators. Kelly instantly began running, trying to catch up with him.

Rowan ran behind her, almost colliding with her as they came to an abrupt stop.

"What are we running for?" Rowan asked.

"I just thought I saw Glen."

"Pardon me?"

"The guy running."

"The guy running had a buzz cut. Glen doesn't have one of those. Not even remotely similar to look at."

"I saw his face for a second. It looked *exactly* like Glen."

"Okay. But we have to get moving right now. If we don't, we're going to miss our flight to Rocky. And if we do that we're both out of a job." Rowan pulled Kelly into motion and they jogged to their departure gate.

Everybody else had already boarded by the time they got there. They ran onto the plane and took their seats.

Rowan buckled her seat belt and stretched her legs out in front of her. "I *love* business class."

"And I *love* travelling with you" Kelly grinned. "It means I actually *get* to travel business class. Otherwise it's cattle class the whole way, baby."

"Yuck," Rowan said. "Too squashy for me."

"Must be fun being a six foot blonde."

Rowan snorted a laugh. "That's one way to put it." She eyed Kelly. "You're not that much shorter than I am, you know."

"I also don't attract as much attention."

"You aren't thought of as a dumb blonde."

"That's just one of the joys of being gorgeous."

Rowan had no rejoinder for that.

The stewardess leant over them. "Coffee?"

"No thank you," Rowan said. She glanced at Kelly, who was shaking her head.

"I hope we catch up with Glen. I'm worried about him," Kelly said.

"Truth? So am I." She hesitated and then looked Kelly square in the eye. "I'm also not good with this entire trip. Feels bad to me."

Kelly's dark eyes flickered with relief. "I know what you mean. I feel like something's not right."

The plane gathered speed as it rocketed down the runway for takeoff. Kelly clutched Rowan's arm.

"I'm sorry," she said, peering at Rowan.

Rowan patted her hand. "That's fine. I don't mind."

As soon as they were in the air, Kelly relaxed and slowly loosened her grip on Rowan's arm.

"Can I ask you something?" Rowan said.

"Sure."

"Who's the mystery woman you had the date with?"

"That would be Genevieve. My soon to be ex, I think."

"Is this mutual?"

Kelly watched her closely. "I think so. I'm just not interested in this anymore. She's giving me a choice between work and her and work is going to win."

"Wow," Rowan said.

Kelly shrugged. "It's okay. I never thought this was going to be long term. We lasted five years, which is surprising in retrospect. Genevieve has never understood that I want a career and our lives would have to accommodate that." The fine edge of old frustration was in Kelly's tone.

"That's why I'm unattached," Rowan said. "I can do both, but I don't like clingy or demanding."

Kelly nodded enthusiastically. "I hear you." She eyed Rowan speculatively. "But you really are incredibly beautiful. I'm surprised you're not taken."

"Who said I wasn't?" Rowan grinned. "I'm not attached but that doesn't mean I'm not taken."

"That doesn't make a lot of sense."

Rowan laughed. "One day you'll get it." She sighed and leant back in her seat. "I hate to be mundane, but we really should talk about this site visit."

"I know," Kelly said. "I printed out driving directions. You were right about the drive. It *is* five hours."

"Yeah. I figure we find a motel just outside Rocky and on the road to Settler's Creek and get most of a night's sleep. We can keep going early in the morning."

"Either that or we just head out when we hit the airport. I know it's a long drive but we'll get more sleep."

"Okay, play it by ear." She turned to Kelly. "Tell me more about this site. Ryan Crossland sounded pissed and that didn't put me in a good position to find out much about anything."

"Well, it's an internal network only. No external interfaces.

That's why we can't do our usual remote thing. It was the whole reason for the site visit. I was dealing with them in a pre-sales capacity and it sounded like their technical crew was pretty good. Ryan Crossland has always been a thorn in our side, though. He's always out of sorts. He's always issuing threats and ultimatums. I tried talking to him a couple of times but I got the distinct impression he didn't have much time for women, because he kept trying to push my buttons. I stepped back and gave it to Glen, and I was supporting him as a point of escalation. After that, we started to get into a rhythm and their entire mood became friendly. Glen came up here for proof of concept. That's what this install is. This is *not* the right place or government department to be going south with."

"If we get in here, we have virtually the whole government. I get all of that. Did Glen show any signs of instability before this visit? Did it look like he needed a break? Had his personal life gone south?"

Kelly was silent for a moment. She slowly shook her head. "Not that I know of. He's always been the same." She looked at Rowan. "Until today, that is."

"Yesterday, technically. One thing I also don't understand is why he didn't check in with you yesterday. That's risky."

"I know that now," Kelly said. "But you have to understand. If you end up in a computer room, nine times out of ten your cell phone doesn't work, and if it does they won't let you use it. This site is worse for that because it's in the middle of nowhere. That was always the beauty of using Glen for installs. He almost never needed help and checking up on him was always unnecessary."

I get that. I've been on more than one site visit myself for an install. "New policy, then," Rowan said. "Now all of our site technicians have to check in on a daily basis when they're out on site. I don't care where they are or how good they are. They have to call in. We're not doing this, this way, ever again."

Kelly nodded. "Understood, Rowan. I'll send out an e-mail blast when we hit the motel."

"Works for me."

"Are you okay to do training?" Kelly asked.

Rowan smirked inwardly and kept a neutral expression. "Of course." She studied Kelly. "Are you calling me a dumb blonde?"

Kelly flushed dark red and appeared to be struggling to form a response.

Rowan finally took pity on her and laughed. "I'm teasing you. I'm fine. We could even swap you know. *I* could do the install and *you* could do the training."

"I didn't realize you remembered how." This time there was a twinkle in Kelly's dark eyes.

"Barely but I'm sure I could manage." Rowan smiled. *We both know I'm as good as Glen is technically.*

"You sure? I'm not sure we still package the comic book version of the instructions."

Rowan snorted a laugh. "Damn. Okay, I changed my mind. I'm screwed."

They both laughed and fell companionably silent.

After a moment, Rowan pulled out her laptop and began to survey her e-mail. Kelly quickly followed suit and they spent the rest of their flying time either rolling their eyes or engaged in quiet discussion about work.

"DO YOU WANT to drive?" Rowan asked as she tossed her luggage into the boot of their rented Ford Falcon.

"Nope." Kelly held the map up. "I'm good to navigate."

Rowan looked at her watch. It was close to eight o'clock. "How are you feeling? You want to go all the way to Settler's Creek this evening or you want to wait until tomorrow morning?"

"Let's just get this done," Kelly said as they got into the car. "There's still plenty of light left."

Rowan nodded and twisted the key in the ignition. The car started with a satisfying purr. She glanced at the fuel gauge. *Full. Good.* "Okay. Where are we going?"

Kelly studied the map for a moment. "We have to get to the Bruce Highway, then take the right fork off onto the Capricorn Highway. We're on that for a while and then we take a right onto

Settler's Creek Road." She frowned. "That's a ways down and we have to be careful of landmarks or we're going to miss it."

Rowan nodded. "Cool. Take us to the Bruce Highway."

"It's right onto Hunter, then left on North, then right onto George. We should bump into it fairly quickly."

"Good. Let's get this show on the road."

They quickly found themselves on the Bruce Highway. They passed lit houses and children walking desultorily down the streets. The late afternoon sunshine beat down unmercifully into the car and Rowan flicked on the air conditioning, but still sweated under her light tank top.

Rowan surreptitiously eyed Kelly as she took off her shirt and tossed it onto the back seat. *Nice body. I would* love *to have that in my hands.* She inwardly shook herself and focused on driving.

After a couple of hours, Rowan pulled over into a darkened service station on an otherwise deserted stretch of empty highway.

Kelly gave her a questioning look.

"I have to stretch my legs," Rowan said. "I think we both need a quick break."

The full moon bathed them both in blue, ghostly light as they stretched. Rowan stretched out her arms and shoulders and caught Kelly staring at her. She feigned ignorance and faced Kelly, hands resting on her hips.

"How far until we hit the turnoff?" Rowan asked.

"Anyone's guess," Kelly said, as Rowan bent over the map with her. "I think we're about here." She tapped a spot on the map.

Rowan nodded. "Yeah, that looks about right. I remember passing this creek."

"Yep," Kelly said. "I figure if we get to here we've gone too far."

"That'll work. We're just under three quarters of a tank. We should be able to absorb bad turns."

Kelly laughed. "I guess so." She looked around into the ghostly darkness. "Kind of plays on your nerves, doesn't it?"

"I've got good company so I'm fine."

Kelly looked directly at her, her face deeply shadowed. "I

never said I wasn't. I'm also enjoying the company. That doesn't mean that I don't feel like we're at the arse end of nowhere."

Rowan laughed softly. "It won't be long until we're crawling back out again. And if it makes you feel any better, our flight back to Sydney is Saturday at two, so we're going to do the drive back in broad daylight."

"So most of Saturday is going to be out of Sydney. Good. I'm done with Genevieve and I'm going to tell her tonight. If I'm lucky she'll be gone by the time I get back."

"You don't want to be there if she cleans you out?"

Kelly shook her head. "She can't take anything that I'm going to miss. I just want out."

Rowan got back into the car, Kelly close behind her. "I hear you."

Rowan pulled out onto the deserted road. After an hour or so they reached the Settler's Creek turnoff.

"That's pretty cool," Kelly said as the headlights flashed on a large green sign that said *Settler's Creek Road.*

Rowan shook her head. "I wasn't expecting that. I was fully expecting to miss the turn off." She made the turn onto Settler's Creek Road.

"Department of Defense is up there. Wouldn't do to have everybody miss it, would it?" Kelly said.

"No, I suppose not."

Thick trees crowded the road and the car's tires hissed over fallen leaves. The leaves swirled gently in the wind. The headlights shone bright and strong onto the road ahead of them, dispelling the darkness.

Rowan glanced at Kelly. Her head lay against the backrest of the seat and she looked as though she was asleep. Rowan longed to brush her fringe out of her eyes and turned away with a sigh.

The wind picked up after half an hour or so. Rowan easily navigated the narrow, twisting road that curved up the side of a mountain. To their right was a plain, bathed in the cold, blue glow of moonlight. The rushing wind made a low, stentorian noise that made her uneasy. She glanced at Kelly—who was awake and looked as tense as she felt—and considered turning on the radio.

She decided against it. The thought of music drowning out the low sounds was somehow worse than the wind itself.

"Are we there yet?" Kelly asked.

Rowan smiled. "Nope. Should be close, though." She frowned at the flash of light through the trees. "Hah. What's that up ahead?"

"You're going to stop, aren't you?" Kelly said.

"I have to," Rowan said. "I'm really tired and I need to stretch my legs."

"If you were tired you should have told me. I would have taken over driving."

God, you're so cute when you blush. "It's fine, Kell. If it was a major problem I'd have told you."

She put out her indicator and pulled into an open, windswept ledge that seemed to be a lookout. She stopped the car and shut off the engine. The headlights cut out and they were bathed in a pallid, orange glow.

Rowan opened the door and stretched out. Her back cracked.

Kelly got out more slowly.

Rowan spotted a small monument over to one side, at the edge of what looked like a drop off. She headed over to it on rubbery legs. She felt numb. *Damn. I am turning into such a bloody wimp. One small road trip and I'm stuffed.*

She was right. The monument was on the edge of a cliff and looked down on a small, silvery township nestled in a stand of trees on a vast plain. A river curved past it on one side.

She bent over and read the monument.

Ithaca, June 20th, 1902
Gone to rest with God
   Here, on this hill and in this valley, lie the remains of the one hundred and twelve souls of Ithaca. Settler's Creek rose out of the ashes, but Ithaca mercifully remains forever a memory.
   Pray for the damned--may they find peace in eternity.

"Wow," Kelly said right next to her ear. "That's one hell of an inscription, isn't it?" She shivered.

Rowan took a deep breath to steady her heart. She shook slightly. "You just scared the crap out of me."

"I'm sorry, Rowan," Kelly said. "I didn't mean to do that."

"It's fine." She looked around the windswept lookout, feeling cold and alone. *This feels like we're the last two people left alive.* "Let's get the hell out of here. I want to get some sleep." She glanced at her watch. It was close to one in the morning.

"I agree," Kelly said. "You want me to drive?"

"Cheeky." Rowan grinned despite herself. "Look at the road. I'm sure we're right on top of Settler's Creek."

Kelly laughed.

They got into the car and Rowan pulled back out onto the deserted road. A minute or so later a speed sign that said *60* appeared and Rowan slowed down. They passed a couple of darkened houses. Lights on the side of the road came into view.

Settler's Creek Motel said a large sign, bathed in white light.

"We're here," Rowan said.

"Are they even open?"

"According to Barb Mitchell they're a twenty-four hour operation," Rowan said.

They pulled up on fresh asphalt under a brand new awning outside new, modern doors marking the entrance to the motel.

A clerk came out of the back room and approached the door.

Kelly looked at Rowan and sighed in relief. "I was half expecting to end up using you as a pillow."

"Sure." Rowan wagged a warning finger in Kelly's face. "No drooling. Rowie don't do no drooling."

Kelly's mouth dropped open. She stared at Rowan, clearly unable to form any coherent reply.

Rowan laughed. "C'mon. Let's get our rooms and get some sleep."

Kelly nodded and followed her to the door the smiling motel clerk held open for them.

CHAPTER 4

ROWAN HAD JUST lay down in bed when there was a soft knock on the door. She got up with a sigh, blinking her stinging eyes.

She pulled back the curtain beside the door. Kelly stood outside, shifting from foot to foot.

"Kell," she said as she pulled the door open. "What's up?"

Kelly's gaze immediately took in her barely clothed form, and then fastened on her face. She blushed.

"I just noticed something."

Rowan raised an eyebrow. "Really?"

Kelly's blush increased. "Uh. Uh. Um. Did you notice there was another car in the parking lot with us?"

Rowan's eyes narrowed. "You think it was Glen? Where is he?"

"No. The car's gone. I got the number plate, though." She held up a small slip of paper.

Rowan glanced around the parking lot, which seemed to be empty of cars besides theirs. "Come in, Kell."

Kelly brushed against her as she stepped into Rowan's room. She stood beside the bed uncertainly.

"Sit down. You're making me tense." Rowan sank into a surprisingly comfortable chair in front of a small desk.

Kelly obediently perched on the bed.

"Talk to me," Rowan said.

"I got the plates and the surround said Rockhampton Avis. It was probably Glen."

"Not so fast, Kell," Rowan said. "First, we don't know if Glen left before we got here. We called him on his cell so there's no way to know where he was. For all we know, he could still be here and just not be in his room. He could be anywhere. Second, there are other rental car companies at the airport. He could have gotten a car from any of them. You don't even know that it was Glen's. It could be anyone's. You don't know who was supposed to be here this week and who wasn't. It could be perfectly innocent." She rubbed her eyes. "Besides, no matter what, we're stuck here for the next three days. We *have* to finish this site visit. Customer first, wayward Glen second."

"Yeah, you're right." Kelly looked abashed. "God, I'm sorry for dragging you out of bed. I was so sure I'd found him."

"No problem. That's what I'm here for."

Kelly got off the bed. "I'm going to go hit the sack. You want me to tuck you in?"

Rowan laughed. "Go to bed. Brat."

Kelly gave her a small salute and left.

Rowan climbed into bed and flicked out the lights. She fell asleep in five minutes, despite her prevailing sense of unease.

ROWAN OPENED HER eyes at eight o'clock the next morning. *Wow. I feel surprisingly good, considering.*

She got out of bed and headed into the shower.

She was mostly dressed when there was a knock on the door.

"If that's you, Kell, come on in," she called, buttoning her blouse.

The door opened and Kelly came in, watching Rowan as she buttoned the last button on her blouse, just over her breasts.

Kelly looked as cool and elegant as ever in her business suit.

"You look terrific," Rowan said, shutting her mouth with a snap.

Kelly smiled at her, eyes raking her from top to bottom. "You can talk, boss. You look amazing."

"Thank you." Rowan smiled. "Is it already hot out there?"

Kelly shook her head. "Not really. Just feels funny."

"What does that mean?"

"You'll see. Or not. Maybe it's just in my head."

Now I have *to see this. This is just so unlike Kelly. Feelings? She's a seasoned professional. She's much more rational and grounded than that.*

"Lead the way." Rowan gestured ahead of her and held the door open for Kelly. Her heart skipped a beat as she caught a whiff of Kelly's perfume. *Wow. She always smells so beautiful. How the hell am I going to last three days out here without kissing her?* Rowan shook herself. *Get your head on straight.*

"Rowan? Are you feeling all right?" Kelly looked concerned.

"I'm fine." Rowan, mustered a smile for her.

Kelly held open the door to reception and they followed the small signs that pointed toward the restaurant and breakfast.

"What are you going to have?" Kelly asked after a waitress ushered them to a seat.

Kelly looked as though she was surrounded by an aura.

Great. I'm getting a migraine on top of everything. "I'm going to go for something light. I'm not really all that hungry."

"I'm going to have to load up," Kelly said. "I imagine I'm going to be stuck in the computer room all day long. No rest for the wicked."

"I won't let them do that to you. If they don't want to let you out of the computer room, I'm coming down to get you."

Kelly gave her a sad smile. "I hope so. I'd love to have lunch with you."

"You will." She nodded toward the buffet. "After you."

Kelly stood, Rowan close behind her. "Since I'm actually going to be fed during the middle of the day, I'm going to go for something light as well. Truth be told, I'm not hungry enough to want to pork up on food today."

"I hear you," Rowan said. She wasn't hungry at all. She forced herself to grab a bagel and some cream cheese.

Kelly followed suit and they went back to their table and two steaming cups of coffee.

Maybe I just need to wake or something. Rowan took a sip of her coffee. It was strong and felt wonderful going down.

Kelly was carefully applying cream cheese to her bagel and Rowan equally carefully watched her. Kelly's long-fingered hands moved swiftly and surely, and with an economy of motion Rowan found intriguing. *She's hot. You're just hot and bothered. Get over it. You're on a business trip and it's bad juju for a boss to get tangled up with a team member.*

Suddenly Kelly stiffened. She was looking out of the bay windows into the parking lot of the restaurant.

"What?" Rowan followed the direction of her gaze. She struggled to remain expressionless. Auras bled and swirled all round everything outside.

Kelly was silent a moment and then shook her head. She looked pale, Rowan noted with interest.

"I'm all right," Kelly said. "I'm not really hungry anymore."

"Let's go. I'm not hungry either." Rowan signed the slip the waitress had left for them and they left the restaurant.

The auras swirled and eddied, and Rowan noted with almost clinical interest that her stomach felt fine.

"You want to head to site?" Kelly asked, shaking her out of her reverie.

Rowan looked at her watch. It was after nine. "Might as well. Maybe they'll be impressed and think we're keen or something."

"I just don't want to work overtime tonight."

"You won't. I promise, Kelly." She pulled Kelly to a halt. "What's up?"

Kelly studied her, her beautiful features still. "I don't know," she said after a moment, frustration evident in her tone. "It's a beautiful day, it's quiet, I smell eucalyptus and for some reason my nerves are shot. I'm nervous as hell."

"Look. If it would make you feel better, I'll try and get down to the computer room during the first break. Give you some moral support or something."

"You don't have to do that. I'm an adult."

"I want to."

Kelly smiled. "Thank you, Rowan. I appreciate it."

Rowan instantly promised herself that she would be down there, come hell or high water, if it would make Kelly smile like that at her again.

"Grab your stuff and let's get going," Rowan said, heading toward her room.

Kelly gave her a quick salute. "Right you are, boss."

"You want to drive this time?" Rowan asked as she tossed her laptop case on the back seat of the car.

"All right. You can see how bad my driving really is."

Rowan grinned and got in the passenger seat. "And you can see how good my back seat driving really is."

Kelly snorted a laugh and twisted the key. The engine instantly started and Kelly expertly pulled out of the spot.

"You know where we're going?" Rowan asked.

"Yep. It's about five minutes down the road. We pass a couple of crescents and then we're there."

They pulled up at a four way intersection. Left went to Ithaca, right to Settler's Creek and straight ahead to Department of Defense.

"One thing I'll give to them," Kelly said as she pulled through the intersection. "They're pretty good with the signage here."

"They certainly are," Rowan said.

They arrived at a three-story ultra-modern office building surrounded by a vast parking lot.

The lot had been freshly asphalted and the line markings looked as though they'd been done in the previous twenty-four hours. It was mostly deserted. Kelly slowly parked in a visitor's parking spot right in front of the doors.

Rowan peered up at the building, struck by how clean and new it looked. Even the landscaping looked as though someone had finished it sometime in the previous week. When she got out she could smell the fresh wood from the wood chips in the neatly manicured garden beds.

"Wowsers," Kelly said softly as they went through the sparkling automatic doors. "Your tax dollars at work."

Rowan snorted a laugh. "And they're being antsy about paying us."

In the center of the vast lobby was a circular receptionist desk. Concrete and glass staircases were close to the walls on either side. They led to the first level. They could see tables against a glass railing, which Rowan thought belonged to a coffee shop on the first level. Scattered people walked up there, some holding coffee, engaged in conversation, and some ambling back to their desks. Soldiers stood unobtrusively and vigilantly as people passed by.

"Can I help you?" the receptionist asked. Her gaze swept over them both.

"We're here to see Ryan Crossland and Victor Hadley," Rowan said with an easy smile. "I'm Rowan May and this is Kelly Carne. We're from Octahedron Software."

The receptionist's lips tightened in displeasure. "Sign in please." She pushed a ledger toward them and handed them both visitor's tags. "Take a seat," she said, indicating chairs and a low coffee table close to them. "I'll page them for you."

"Thank you," Rowan said. She went to the chairs and took a seat on the sofa, Kelly beside her.

"Are you feeling any better?" Rowan asked softly.

Kelly looked tense. "Nope."

"I'll check up on you. Promise."

"Thanks, boss." Kelly mustered a strained smile for Rowan.

Rowan opened her mouth to speak as two men approached them. One was short and fat, his bald spot covered by a carefully waxed comb over. Expensive, cloying aftershave hovered over him like a noxious cloud. His gaze swept Rowan from top to bottom, lingering on her breasts and hips. A smile twitched around his lips. Rowan struggled with the urge to slap him.

The man behind him was tall and thin. His collar length hair looked windblown. He had large, wire frame glasses and had an air of harmless stupidity about him. *I can understand why Glen would have been annoyed by him but I don't know why he would have been openly rude.*

"I'm Ryan Crossland," the short man said. "This is Vic Hadley." He held out his hand and Rowan gamely took it. He squeezed her hand and then covered it with his free hand.

"Nice to meet you," Rowan said, trying and failing to retrieve her hand. *Be nice, Rowan. Just be nice.*

Kelly and Victor both murmured their greetings.

"You're early," Victor said.

"We wanted to see how far Glen had gotten," Kelly said.

Rowan snuck a glance at her. Her dark eyes glittered with anger.

"Actually, that's not a bad idea," Rowan said smoothly.

"We're running a day behind on the installation, so maybe you'd better show us where the server is. We should get started."

Ryan pursed his lips. "That's getting right into it. I take it you'll be doing the training, Rowan?"

Rowan nodded, looking down at him. She gave him a winning smile. "Certainly will."

His eyes travelled over her breasts.

"Come on then." He nodded toward Victor. "You want to show Kelly the computer room?"

"No problem," Victor smiled at Kelly. "The lifts are this way." He indicated the rear, shadowed wall behind the receptionist's desk.

"And you can come with me." Ryan smiled at Rowan.

Rowan smiled back. *This is going to be a* very *long morning.* She took shallow breaths and followed him to the stairs.

KELLY TRAILED BEHIND Victor to the lifts, fighting down a surge of helpless jealousy at the way Ryan kept pawing at her beautiful boss. *I want her to want me to do that to her. I wish she wasn't straight. She probably doesn't mind. Maybe she can smooth things over with him, since she likely doesn't mind the way he interacts with her. She must be used to it. I can't help it. He's such a jerk. How could anyone in their right mind treat Rowan--of all people--like that? Wonder if they treat everyone like idiots? No wonder Glen got the shits quickly with this place.*

"—trip up here?" Victor stabbed the button for the elevator.

"Pardon?" Kelly asked, distracted by Rowan's beautiful behind disappearing up the stairs.

"I said, how was the trip up here?"

"It was good. Long. But easy to find."

Victor laughed and stepped aside as the lift doors opened. "Heard that once or twice before." He hit the button for the first sub-basement.

"Underground?" Kelly said.

"So there's less chance of it getting destroyed if we get bombed."

"Only one level? Don't you have to be deeper for that?"

"I was kidding."

"Oh."

The car slid to a halt and the doors opened onto a darkened hallway. A shadowed computer room lay ahead of them, encased in glass. It was cold.

This place is really creepy, but I can't see that Glen would have lost his nerve. It's just dark. And creepy.

Victor led the way out of the lift and through small pools of light that flickered into being as they approached. He quickly swiped his magnetic key and the door beeped and clicked open. He stood aside and Kelly entered.

"This place is huge," she said.

"Yeah. Was for the old PABX which took up most of a room." He led the way toward the server rack. The lights flickered on ahead of him. The rest of the room remained in darkness.

"Building's pretty new for something that had an old PABX."

"It burnt down a couple of years ago. They finished rebuilding it last year."

"Really? I never heard that."

"You wouldn't have. We're just a government department, not much else."

"Fair enough."

They came to a stop in front of a server rack. The door was slightly open and a suit coat lay draped over the top of it. *That has to be Glen's coat. Why on earth did he leave it down here? Did something happen?*

Victor pulled out a tray holding a keyboard and mouse. He flicked a switch and unlocked the computer. He rapidly hit some keys.

"Got that? That's the password for this account."

"Is it a domain admin?"

"Yes, it is."

"May I?" Kelly gestured toward the keyboard. She felt herself beginning to relax.

"Sure," Victor said.

She opened windows explorer and examined the directory

structure. *There's nothing here. Glen didn't do anything. What did he do all day?*

"I'd like to apologize for Glen's behavior." Kelly looked Victor in the eye. "It was unprofessional. We'll be having words about it."

Victor frowned. "*Having* words? You mean you haven't seen him yet?"

Kelly shook her head. "We didn't even know there was a problem until Ryan called Rowan."

Victor's mouth tightened and she saw anger flash in his eyes. His impassive mask quickly slipped back into place. "He was a raving maniac. I had to go to a meeting and he was gone by the time I got back."

You left him alone down here? Oh, crap. This really is *going to be a shitty site visit.*

"Did he say anything to you before he left?"

"He was raving about the lift and bright lights. I left him here and he was gone by the time I got back."

"Did anyone see him leave?"

"Nope."

"Once again, I'd like to apologize. I can't imagine what got into him."

"He needs a mental health professional."

Kelly simply stared at him. He held her gaze for a moment, and then his eyes stuttered away from her face. Kelly sensed that he was hiding something.

Victor glanced at his watch. "I'm going to duck upstairs for a few minutes and I'll be back down. Would you like me to get you anything? Will you be all right until I get back?"

"No, I'm fine and I'll be okay."

Victor nodded and left her. She watched the lights flicker on ahead of him.

Kelly turned back to the server with a sigh. *This is going to be one long morning.*

CHAPTER 5

ROWAN WAITED PATIENTLY as the last of the training attendees filtered into the room and slid into seats. Ryan Crossland sat behind her.

"Rowan, would you like to go out to dinner this evening?" Ryan asked.

Rowan glanced at him as his gaze openly lingered on her breasts.

"Sure. Kelly and I would love to take you up on that." Rowan smiled. "Can we do it when we finish up today? We had a long trip and both of us would like an early night." She felt a shot of vicious pleasure as irritation flickered in his eyes.

"Yes, of course."

Victor ducked through the doorway behind the last of the stragglers. He waved quickly at them and took an unobtrusive seat at the side of the room.

"Good morning, everyone," Rowan said. "My name is Rowan May. I'm the Director of Technical Services for Octahedron Software. I'm up here to show you how our monitoring software works. Before we get started, I'd like to know a little bit more about you. How about we go around the room and introduce ourselves and give a quick overview of what each of us does." She looked at the mousy woman sitting next to her. "Would you like to kick us off?"

KELLY WATCHED AS the installation continued. She glanced at her watch. *That'll probably take another fifteen minutes or so.*

She looked up at the coat slung over the cabinet door. She carefully took it down and rifled through the pockets for the third time. *Empty.* She sighed in frustration. *I don't know if that's normal or not.* She looked around on the floor, careful to move so the sensors turned on extra lights. *Nothing. No sign of his briefcase. If he was in a hurry I could see him grabbing his laptop and leaving his jacket behind.*

She bent down and peered at the computer screen. The percentage counter seemed stuck on ninety percent.

It's not normal for Glen to have left his coat behind. Wonder if he left anything else behind?

She bent down and looked around the server racks, shivering at the blast of cold air that came from the floor vents.

Nothing. The floor around the racks was empty.

The room was nestled in darkness and only the three lights above the narrow passage between the racks provided any kind of illumination. She suppressed a shudder. *Of all places to be left alone, it had to be here.*

The hair on the back of her neck rose and flashes of light quickly filtered into her vision. She looked down at her hands and saw auras bleeding into each other around them.

Shit.

She glanced at the computer screen again. The installation was *still* sitting at ninety percent. She studied the screen, unwilling to look around.

She was suddenly bathed in light. She looked up, heart hammering, and saw that the lights over the adjacent passage of server racks had gone on.

Shrug it off, Kell. You're a professional. "Is there someone there?"

Silence.

It took all of her courage, but she managed to take a step sideways and duck down so she could see through the servers to the next row over.

Her heart rate doubled and a slow wave of terror rolled over her.

A reflection of a tall man in fatigues was visible in the glass doors on the other side of the rack mount. The metallic taste of fear flooded her mouth and she forced herself to look around.

She couldn't see anyone who would have been able to create the reflection, and yet there he was, staring at her disapprovingly.

She shivered and took a step back.

The lights in the other passage went out and she took an involuntary step back, shaking. Her back bumped up against the glass doors of a server rack. Adrenaline flooded her system.

"Who is it?" she said again, amazed at how calm she sounded.

No answer.

No footsteps.

No sign of the man in fatigues.

Christ, I wish Victor would just get himself back here.

Just at that moment, there was a click and the door to the computer room opened.

Kelly remained rooted to the spot, unable to move.

Footsteps entered the room and got louder as they came closer.

Her eyes widened and she shook as they came down the passageway.

A tall, familiar figure filled her vision. Long, blonde hair, carefully tied back. Bright, cornflower blue eyes set in classically beautiful features. A curvy, womanly figure and a plunging neckline that revealed the cleft of her full breasts.

Rowan. It was Rowan.

And Victor was behind her.

The smile slipped away from her beautiful face and she eyed Kelly with considerable alarm. "Kell? Are you all right? You look like you've seen a ghost."

Kelly wanted to throw herself into Rowan's arms a squeeze tight.

"Do you want some water?" Victor asked as Rowan approached her.

"Yes, please." Kelly shook with the aftermath of her terror.

"Okay," Victor said with his banal smile. "I'll be back in a jiffy."

He turned and left them.

Rowan glanced over her shoulder. "He's gone." She turned back to Kelly. "Hey, is everything all right? You really do look terrible."

"I've never been so glad to see anyone in my entire life," Kelly said. "You're a sight for sore eyes. It's so *creepy* down here."

Rowan nodded sympathetically. "We can swap, if you like? I'll finish the install and you can do the training."

"*No. No way* am I letting you do that."

Rowan's eyebrows shot skyward at her tone.

"Don't pull rank on me, Rowan," Kelly said. "I won't let you do it. The install is *my* problem. Let me deal with it."

"Uh, okay. Hey, you're shaking." Rowan gently put her hands on Kelly's upper arms, steadying her. She gazed into Kelly's eyes. "What happened, Kell? You're really shook up."

Kelly looked deep into Rowan's eyes. She felt like she was drowning. Rowan's gentle grip, her calm, and her solid strength began to seep into Kelly and she found herself relaxing.

"I'm okay." She mustered a smile. "You've been around Ryan too long. I can smell his aftershave."

Rowan's straight, white teeth flashed in a grin. "And it's only going to get worse. He invited me to dinner tonight."

Kelly's lips tightened and she hoped that none of the jealousy she felt showed on her face. "Nice."

"I'm glad you think so." Rowan snorted a laugh. "You're coming."

"Really? I think I'm allergic to him." Kelly mustered a smile. "Besides, I think he's more interested in getting into your pants than mine."

Rowan stared at her. "Really? He could do two for the price of one."

Kelly gaped at her. She saw the twinkle in Rowan's eyes. She laughed, despite herself.

The door clicked open and a few seconds later Victor rounded the corner holding a bottle of water. Rowan released her arms. Victor held the water out to Kelly and she took it with a murmured thanks.

Kelly took a swig of the water and felt her nerves begin to settle again. Rowan watched her, concerned.

"I'm good," Kelly said softly to her. She glanced at the computer screen. The installation was finished. She looked at Victor. "You have to stay down here with me. Now I need some help with the configuration."

"Do you want to do that from my desk? We can remote into the machine."

Now he tells me. "Sure. I'll just grab my laptop and we can go up."

Victor led the way out of the computer room, Rowan close behind him. Kelly brought up the rear, her laptop bag in one hand with Glen's suit coat draped over it.

Kelly was seeing auras again by the time they reached the door. She felt sick. As they stepped out into the darkened corridor, she heard a soft ding, almost the sound of an elevator, in the opposite direction to the one they'd used to come down.

Rowan glanced back at her and Kelly knew by the look in her eyes that she'd heard it as well. She shook her head slightly. Rowan gave an almost imperceptible nod. Kelly knew she would be expecting to hear later why Kelly was asking for her silence.

They got out of the lift on the first floor and Rowan headed back to the training room, while Kelly trailed Victor to his office.

ROWAN WATCHED KELLY follow Victor. Her arms tingled with the urge to pull her in close. *I wonder what could possibly have happened to her to make her look like that? I've never seen her panic or get scared about anything.*

"Okay, everyone." She surveyed the room full of people. "Let's get into it again."

They broke for lunch an hour later, and Rowan closed her notebook as Ryan approached with an ingratiating smile.

"Would you like to come down to the cafeteria for lunch?" Ryan said.

No way. "Sure," Rowan said. "Let's just swing by Kelly and Victor. I want to make sure they're on track."

"Of course. Follow me."

Ryan led the way to Victor's office. The door was open and Ryan quickly knocked as they walked in. Victor's office was a study in neatness and order. On almost every surface there were model planes, and on the wall was a reproduction of the Red Baron in a dogfight with English planes.

Kelly and Victor remained bent over, studying Kelly's laptop.

"Kell," Rowan said.

Kelly and Victor remained engrossed.

"Kelly," Rowan said a little louder and they both looked up.

Kelly looked surprised. "Hi."

"You want to grab some lunch?" Rowan asked.

Kelly glanced at Victor. He shook his head. "I'm good, I brought mine in with me today."

Jerk. "Kell, you want to join us?"

"No, I'm fine. I really should get this done," Kelly said. "If you don't mind working through lunch, Vic?"

Victor shook his head. "We're on a roll. Let's get this done?"

Rowan nodded, and Ryan waved them goodbye and took them to the cafeteria. It was crowded around the counter, but Ryan pushed through to the front of the queue, garnering them some nasty stares. They ordered—salad for Rowan, a thick, tuna sandwich for Ryan—and found a seat at the side of the room.

"Do you like our little town?" Ryan asked.

No. "Yes I do." Rowan waved her fork around, indicating the room. "I have to admit I find this building to be quite a surprise. It looks out of place in the pastoral surroundings."

Ryan smiled. "The government built this place out of the way for a reason. And we got them to build us something more than a bark shack."

Rowan laughed, despite herself. "It's lovely."

"And state of the art. What you're in now are just basically a collection of admin offices. Nothing else here. Projects are closer to Toowoomba."

"So it's just these three floors and the basement computer room?"

Ryan nodded. "Yes." He frowned. "Despite what Glen seemed to think."

Ryan looked annoyed and Rowan braced herself for his venting. "What did Glen say to you?"

"You'd have to ask Victor for chapter and verse. It's pretty much what I told you. He asked where the rear lift in the computer room went to and when Vic told him there wasn't one, he got angry. Then he started raving about lights and sound. Vic left him alone for five minutes and by the time he got back, Glen was gone."

"So you never actually saw Glen leave the building?"

Ryan shook his head. "No. He *had* to have left because there's nowhere to go except to the places you've been. It's not like we have any hidden rooms here."

Rowan nodded and ate another bite of her salad. *So he's gone, and no one saw him go.*

They ate the rest of their lunch, chatting about nothing. When they got up to leave, Rowan nodded toward the counter. "I'm going to get Kelly something to eat."

Ryan gave her an odd look and she sighed internally. *I'd forgotten how silly customers can sometimes be on a site visit. Thank God today is more than half over.*

KELLY LOOKED UP at the knock on the door. Rowan stood there, holding out a Styrofoam container and a fork.

"Lunch," she said.

Kelly gave her a broad, genuine smile. "Thanks, boss." Her stomach grumbled as if on cue.

The both looked down at her midsection and laughed.

"I'll come and get you at around five," Rowan said.

Kelly remembered that they were having dinner with Ryan and felt a quick blast of dislike which she carefully pushed back. "Sounds good to me."

Rowan nodded and left the office behind Ryan. He put his hand in the small of her back and steered her from the room. Kelly felt another shot of irritation. *God, he's so* annoying.

"You want to eat?" Victor asked, breaking her out of her reverie.

"Yes, please," Kelly said, pulling open the container. *Pasta salad. Rowan, I love you.* She took a few forkfuls of salad.

She looked at the network map on her laptop screen. All of the servers were showing slow response times. She sighed in frustration.

"What's up?" Victor asked.

"For some reason, all the machines are showing a pretty heavy latency." She tapped a small icon of a computer on the screen. "Like that one."

"Well, that's half of the reason we're going to buy your software." Victor shrugged. "The servers are on an automatic reboot tonight. How about if we see if the latency is still there tomorrow? If it is, we'll use your software to try and nail down what it is."

Kelly nodded. "Sounds reasonable." She ate more of her salad.

"Let's just keep going with the config. We can at least set things up the way we want them to be, right?"

"Sure."

They went back to studying Victor's screen.

ROWAN WALKED INTO the training room, Ryan almost glued to the back of her.

I swear I'm going to hear a Velcro tearing sound and his eyes are going to come out of his head and stick to my butt or my boobs. Wow, wait. Look at this. Where the hell did all these people come from?

The room seemed choked. There was the same set of faces from the morning, scattered throughout the crowd of what seemed about fifty people. Half of the newcomers looked as though they'd walked out of a fifties car commercial. Not a hair was out of place, makeup was perfectly applied, shirts were pressed, and trousers sensibly creased. Amongst those were immaculately groomed scientific types wearing lab coats.

Rowan tried not to start. Heavily armed guards stood by the doors and officers nestled themselves unobtrusively along the walls behind some people.

"Rowan."

"Huh?"

"*Rowan*," Ryan said.

"Oh. Yes?" She tried a smile on for him, dimly amazed he wasn't undressing her with his eyes.

"Are you all right, dear?" Ryan actually looked *concerned.*

Rowan blinked. The faces that hadn't been in training in the morning vanished.

Holy cow, what the hell is going on here? I can't say anything or he's going to think I'm nuts.

"I'm good. Just after lunch sleepy."

The crowd—who had also been looking at her askance—seemed to relax.

She smiled at them. "Okay, where did we leave off?"

CHAPTER 6

"THANK GOD TODAY'S over," Kelly said with a sigh as she slid into the driver's seat.

Rowan grinned at her. "So am I. We're right on track with the training. How's the install going?"

"I'm seeing a lot of errors in the network. The servers are on an auto reboot schedule for tonight so we're going to see how things are going tomorrow morning."

She pulled out of their parking spot and slowly rolled up to Ryan, nestled in his Jaguar. She felt a quick shot of dislike and suppressed it.

"I know you're not looking forward to this," Rowan said. "It's only another hour or so. Trust me. I'll get us out of there."

By giving him the lap dance he so clearly wants? Kelly bit off the thought before she could vocalize it.

They followed Ryan's car back to the four-way stop sign. He turned left and they went down a narrow, winding road to the small township of Settler's Creek.

They pulled up into a parking lot behind a small, Chinese restaurant.

"Hope the food's good," Rowan said.

"The company won't be," Kelly muttered.

"Kell, relax. Trust me. It'll be over quickly."

"If you say so, boss."

Kelly followed Rowan out of the car and up to Ryan, who was waiting for them.

"This is one of the better restaurants in town," he said as they approached.

"I believe you," Rowan said as he held the door open for them.

A smiling hostess led them over to a small table under a reproduction of classic Chinese artwork, complete with Chinese characters travelling up one side of it.

Ryan steered Rowan into her chair. *So it begins.* Kelly gritted her teeth and remained quiet as his gaze crawled over Rowan's breasts. All through the meal Rowan laughed at his banal jokes and seemed completely oblivious to his patronizing mannerisms and loose eyes. Kelly remained silent, only speaking when spoken to. She focused on the food. Ryan was right. It really *was* good. Kelly was tense by the end of the meal but her mood never tipped over into foul.

Ryan paid the bill and they left.

"Thank you, Ryan," Rowan said as he walked them over to their car. She gently extracted the keys from Kelly and allowed Ryan to open her door. Kelly got into the passenger side, barely refraining from folding her arms and sticking out her lower lip.

"I'll see you two ladies tomorrow," Ryan said with another ingratiating smile and a small wave.

"Yes, you will," Rowan called back as they drove away.

They were silent as Rowan navigated the narrow road back up the hill to their motel.

"Are you going to talk to me or are you going to keep your mouth shut and frown?" Rowan asked.

"I'm sorry, boss," Kelly said. "I just hate that guy's guts, that's all."

Rowan studied her for a moment. "Look, why don't you get out of your monkey suit and come over to my room? We need to talk about today."

"Okay," Kelly said.

Rowan smiled. "Nothing bad, Kelly."

All Kelly wanted to do was escape. She needed a few minutes to regroup and call Rich. "Give me ten, then, and I'll be there."

Rowan nodded and disappeared into her room.

Kelly let herself into her motel room with a sigh, tossing her laptop and Glen's coat onto the bed. She picked up her cell. *Reception's good. Nice.* She dialed Rich's cell phone from her contacts list and he answered after a couple of rings. Kelly began to change her clothes.

"Boss, hey, how'd it go?" Rich asked. He sounded happy.

"Went well. How were things there today?"

"Quiet. No fires to put out. Just logs to study and e-mails to be sent."

"I don't suppose you've heard from Glen, have you?"

"Nope. Haven't seen him either. I tried calling him around lunch. Only got his voicemail."

"Good. I'm glad you called. Let me know if he *does* answer you."

"I will, boss. Have a good one."

"You too, Rich."

She hung up and pulled a tank top over her head. *Better than my monkey suit.*

She left her room with a sigh and knocked on Rowan's door.

It opened seconds later. Rowan was in her jeans and wore a revealing tank top that clung lovingly to her large breasts. She was barefoot and her long hair hung loose down her back, stripping years off her beautiful features.

Jesus wept. This just gets worse for me all the time. Kelly forced her eyes to Rowan's face. Rowan was grinning.

She flopped down onto the chair and accepted the beer that Rowan thrust in her direction. Rowan perched herself on the end of the bed.

"Cheers," Rowan said as their bottles clinked together.

Kelly took a long swallow of her cold beer, feeling it as it went down. "Oh my God. That tastes *fantastic*." She took another swig.

"Glad you like it." Rowan took her own swallow. "Now suppose you tell me what happened today?"

Kelly felt some of her tension return. "Ryan Crossland annoys the living shit out of me. Victor is a smart guy but a complete idiot. That computer room is as creepy as hell." She shivered, remembering the reflection.

"Hey, hey, hey." Rowan stood and pulled Kelly to her feet. She slipped her arms around Kelly and pulled her in close. Kelly took a deep breath of her perfume and held on tight.

After a too short time, Rowan pulled back and looked into her eyes. "I know Ryan bothers you a lot. Don't let it. I'm keeping him happy, that's all."

Kelly felt her face heat. She hadn't meant to be so transparent. "I'm sorry. I'm not normally like this," she mumbled. "It's been a hell of a day."

"I know it has." Rowan sat on the edge of the bed and pulled Kelly down beside her. "Now. You want to tell me why this was so bad for you?" Her eyes were gentle and kind.

"The install was pretty straightforward. It's done. Most of the config is done. Should be completely finished by lunch tomorrow. I found Glen's coat in the computer room but no sign of his briefcase or anything else. I called Rich and he hasn't heard from Glen either."

"Okay. First, congratulations. You were awesome at site today. I think you might have fixed our tarnished image with Victor at least. I'm also impressed you were able to get mostly finished so quickly. I think we'll probably be able to leave here early." She smiled. "So that's well and truly under control. Now, what *really* happened?"

"IthinkIsawaghostinthecomputerroom." Kelly felt her face heat again.

"Excuse me?"

"I'm not nuts or overworked, I swear I'm not."

"I didn't think either one. You just told me you thought you saw a ghost in the computer room. Right?"

Kelly's gaze dropped and she studied the carpet, humiliation complete.

"Hey, Kell. Look at me."

Kelly remained silent and engrossed in the carpet's pattern.

"Come on, now, Kell. Look at me." Rowan gently bumped her shoulder.

Kelly took a deep breath and looked at Rowan's beautiful face. Her eyes were kind and gentle.

"Better. Do I look like I don't believe you? You think I didn't hear the ding from *another* lift on that floor? Yes. I heard it. Yes. I think something weird is going on here."

Kelly breathed a sigh of relief. "I *know* what I saw. I *did* see a guy in fatigues."

"You what?"

Kelly told her exactly what she'd seen. Rowan was silent for a long moment after she was finished.

Rowan shook her head. "I don't know that it was a ghost."

"You don't believe me?"

"I never said that and I wouldn't have. You're the most levelheaded person I know. You're more grounded than most people. You can keep calm when everyone around you is going nuts. So no. When you tell me you saw something, I believe it." She smiled at Kelly and took a sip of her beer. "You want me to tell you what *I* saw today?"

Kelly shook with relief at Rowan's reaction. *I should have known she wouldn't go all wiggy on me. Rowan's never been like that. She's the gentlest, kindest and fairest person I've ever met. I hope she's* always *somewhere in my life. She's more than my boss and eye candy. She's my friend.*

"Shoot."

"Aside from the lift, I've been seeing auras all day long. And flashes of light that are like lightning. I don't have a migraine and I'm not prone to them anyway. When we came back from lunch and went back into the training room, it looked as though there were twice as many people in there than should have been. Most of them were transparent. I blinked and it went away. It wasn't double vision. They were distinctly different people."

Kelly didn't know what to think about that. "That's really weird."

Rowan nodded. "I know." She studied Kelly for a moment. "I'm pulling rank for tomorrow. *I'm* going to help Vic. *You're* going to do training."

"Oh, hell *no*, Rowan. I'm *not* letting you do that."

"I'm not giving you the choice," Rowan said softly. "That's what pulling rank means."

"I don't want anything bad to happen to you." Kelly looked directly into Rowan's bright, blue eyes. "I couldn't . . . no way."

"I'll be fine. I'm a big girl."

Yes, you most certainly are. That's one tiny fact that's never *flown right past me.*

"Yes, I know that. I suppose it'll give you some relief from Ryan."

"Can you handle him?"

"It's not *my* boobs he's staring at. I'm not competition for you."

"It's the dumb blonde thing. You're female. He'll try hitting on you eventually."

"I'll just tell him I'm into girls if he tries it."

Rowan laughed. "I'd pay to see that. I'm sure he'd just take that as more of a challenge than a refusal."

They laughed.

"What do you think is going on here, Rowan?" Kelly asked, her sense of unease filtering into her consciousness again.

Rowan was silent for a moment. "This is what we know. We came to site and both of us feel as though the world just isn't right. Like something bad is about to happen and we don't know what. It's setting both of us on edge. We also know that we sent someone up here who was a competent, steady, reliable support technician. He went insane at site—despite never showing any signs of instability before—and ran like hell. You're seeing things and *I'm* seeing things."

"Yeah, that'd be it in a nutshell," Kelly said. "Do you think Ryan and Victor have anything to do with this?"

"I have no idea. How do we know that this isn't some huge government project that's spilling out of containment?"

"We don't." Kelly smiled. "But saying that makes my unreality meter kick in."

"Doesn't it?" Rowan sighed. "All I know is that I want to find Glen. I want to know what pushed him over the edge. I want to know what he *saw*."

"So do I," Kelly said.

Rowan abruptly stood. "I feel really restless. You want to go for a drive?"

"Sure," Kelly said. "Where do you want to go?"

"Mystery tour. You game?"

Rowan grinned and nodded. "Sure."

"Let's go."

"WOW," ROWAN SAID as they pulled into a deserted parking lot close to the edge of the ridge. All around them was a panorama of trees and plain below the ridgeline and sky.

"Yeah," Kelly said. "I saw this when we were headed to site this morning."

Rowan pointed toward the small path that was chained off at the edge of the parking lot.

"I want to see where that goes." She glanced at Kelly, trying not to notice how her muscles stood out in sharp relief under her smooth, creamy skin.

"I'm there." Kelly got out of the car. Rowan felt Kelly's eyes on her.

"Penny for your thoughts, Kell." *Is Kelly blushing?*

"You don't want to know. They're too pedestrian."

They walked along a sandy track to the remains of an old fire pit nestled under an anemic tree. A small monument lay off to one side.

Rowan went over to it.

Ithaca 1850 - 1902. God rest their souls, it said.

"That's depressing, isn't it?" Kelly said directly into her ear. She was so close Rowan felt the warmth from her body.

She looked over her shoulder into Kelly's dark eyes. "Yeah, it is." She smiled. "You're very beautiful."

"So are you," Kelly whispered, leaning into her and kissing her.

Rowan pulled Kelly into her arms, deepening the kiss. She felt Kelly's hands gently stroking her back.

She rested her forehead against Kelly's when they broke. She felt content. "What was that for?"

"Because I think you're the best boss a girl could ever have."

Rowan snorted a laugh. "I sincerely hope you don't do that with all your managers."

"Just you." Kelly kissed her again. "You have no idea how long I've been wanting to do that."

"For as long as I have?"

Kelly pulled back, the dying light of the day giving her skin a golden glow. "You're not straight, are you?"

Rowan laughed outright. "No. You finally noticed?"

Kelly blushed. "I never thought I'd get this lucky. I'm *very* attracted to you, Rowan."

"And I'm *very* attracted to you," Rowan said. "I never thought you paid any attention to me. It wasn't until I realized you were checking out my butt today that I thought I'd have a chance with you."

Kelly blushed harder. "Noticed that, did you?"

"When you looked like you wanted to kill Ryan for staring at my breasts, yes."

Kelly laughed and caressed Rowan's face. "I *hate* the way he does that to you."

Rowan gently trapped her hand against her face and leant into her touch. "I know you do." She smiled. "I don't belong to him." She kissed Kelly again, mind fuzzy with bliss and loving the way Kelly's body felt pressed against the length of hers.

"We have to be careful about *us*," Kelly said. "This is a major conflict of interest."

"Don't worry about it," Rowan said. "I guess it's time to tell you. I got offered another job with Gadgets Inc. I'm going to take it."

"Oh, geez," Kelly said sadly. "I'm going to miss you."

"No, you're going to see me all the time. If you're interested as well, of course. I want to explore *us*."

"*Yes*. I'm interested. God, so do I. I want to keep going with this," Kelly breathed, squeezing Rowan as hard as she could. "I don't want a life that doesn't have you in it."

"Neither do I."

"I'm going to break up with Genevieve when we get back. I was going to do that anyway. It's not working for me."

"I was going to ask you about that. I didn't want you to cheat on her with me."

"I'm not a cheat, Rowan."

"I'm glad." She took Kelly's hand and pulled her into motion.

Kelly pulled in close to her. "We have to talk about *us* and how we're going to handle things."

They reached the car and Rowan unlocked the doors. "I know. We have plenty of time to talk. Do you think we can finish at site tomorrow?"

"If we go until six we should be able to make it."

"Okay, let's do that. I'm going to tell David tomorrow when we're done that we want to stay for Friday just to make sure they're okay. That'll give us a day together before we have to go back and face the real world."

"You want to vacation *here*? Can't we just get the hell out of here?"

"Not so much vacation, although I will admit I'd love to take you out on a date tomorrow evening." Rowan smiled. "You know we can't leave. We *have* to stay to finish up. We have to be professionals."

"All right, we'll stay." Kelly nodded, unconvinced. "I'm there. I'd love to go on a date with you."

"On Friday you and I can spend some time together, plus we're going to have to look for Glen. I don't like this place and I think he—and we—are in a whole mess of trouble."

"What makes you say that?"

"Come with me," Rowan said as they pulled into a parking spot outside Rowan's room at the motel. "I want to show you something."

CHAPTER 7

KELLY GOT OUT of the car and studied Rowan's perfect profile. *Wow. I never thought I'd get this lucky. She's so hot and she's such a sweetie.*

Rowan waited for her and they went to the motel office. Rowan held the door open for her and they went in.

The motel reception was dusty and a peculiar mix of old and new. The bright yellow Formica desk was new, the bell resting on it old and scratched. There was a motel ledger sitting on the counter top and pigeon holes and a rack of keys on the wall behind it. There was no sign of a computer.

Kelly frowned. *That's weird. Where are all the electronics? Are we still in the dark ages?*

Rowan hit the bell on the desk. It dinged loudly and a bald man wearing a polo shirt and a cardigan came out of the back room. His glasses slipped down his nose and he pushed them back up again.

"Help you?" he said.

"Yes," Rowan said. "Do I have any messages? Room four."

The man checked the pigeon holes. "No."

"Okay, thanks."

Kelly stayed close behind Rowan as they left, surreptitiously eyeing the carpet squares on the floor. She followed Rowan back to her room. Rowan let herself in and grabbed a small pyramid of cardboard off the desk.

"Wi fi." She tapped it and tossed it back onto the desk.

"I'm not quite getting you," Kelly said.

"This place is weird. He didn't raise an eyebrow when I asked if I had messages. Why would I bother in the age of smart phones and laptops? They have wifi. There's no computer in reception, just one of those big books they used to use before computers came into wide use."

"Yeah, I'd kind of noticed that." Kelly sat on the edge of the bed. "He was dressed like a refugee from the fifties. This motel is brand new but reception is decked out like it would be if they were moving into the seventies. What the hell is going on here?"

"I don't know." Rowan perched on the bed beside her. She looked at Kelly and Kelly could see the disquiet in her eyes.

"You think we walked into some kind of a ghost story?" Kelly asked.

"I'm not sure what I think yet. It's like we're in the twilight zone."

"Wonder if that's why Glen left like the hounds of hell were on his arse?"

"I'm not sure he's gone," Rowan said. He's booked into room twelve."

"How do you know that?"

"I snuck a look at the ledger when I was getting our beer."

"How dishonest of you."

Rowan snorted a laugh. "I didn't see a checkout date or time. God knows, but I think getting into his room and sneaking a look wouldn't be a bad idea."

"You want to do that now?"

"I'm tempted."

"Why don't we stop being tempted and just do it. His room number was twelve, right?"

Rowan nodded. "Yep."

"Let's go, then."

They left Rowan's room and Kelly felt Rowan's hand slip into hers. They walked along the L-shaped walkway, looking at the room numbers as they went past.

"Nine," Rowan said softly.

"I hate to tell you this," Kelly said. "But it doesn't look like there's going to be a room eleven, let alone a twelve."

Rowan pulled her to a halt and frowned.

Kelly glanced at her and saw her eyes flicker with something that scared Kelly more than she wanted to admit.

"Oh, hell," Rowan said softly.

Kelly shook her head. "Come on, be logical. This could be anything. The other reasonable explanations are that you read the room number wrong or that the clerk wrote it down wrong."

"No one's been at this motel for a while," Rowan said sadly. "Glen, I are the only ones that have stayed here in the last couple of weeks. The rooms all have bay windows at the front. There are curtains. Whose curtains—besides yours and mine—are closed?"

Kelly glanced around. It was hard to see in the darkness. "All the lights in the rooms are off. Let's go back the way we came and see which rooms have closed curtains."

They walked back and peered into all the windows. All the rooms seemed to be empty. They walked past their rooms and checked the first three.

"All empty, Kell," Rowan said. "They're all empty."

"And the motel lights aren't that crash hot. I can't really see into the rooms." Kelly felt uneasy and struggled to push it down.

Rowan let them into her room and they sat down on the bed, side by side, legs stretched out in front of them.

"I feel like we're in the twilight zone." Rowan groped on the bedside table for a moment. She frowned. "Where's the remote?"

Kelly laughed, despite her prevailing sense of disquiet. "Don't look at me. I didn't take it."

"I put it here last night. And it's not here." Her eyebrows drew together as she stared at the television set. "And that would probably be because that television set doesn't *use* a remote."

"Huh?" Kelly peered closely at the television. It had a rounded screen and a large dial to change the television channels. There was an on/off switch and volume control. "Fuck. That thing looks like it's a refugee from the seventies as well." She began to lever herself off the bed. "No biggie. I think I can work out how to make it go."

Rowan instantly held her arm. "Don't, Kell."

"Don't you want to know?" Kelly patted Rowan's hand. "Better to know that not know."

Rowan bit her lip and nodded after a few seconds.

Kelly pulled herself off the bed with a decisiveness she didn't feel and pulled the on/off switch on the television. She realized with distant amazement that her hands were steady. She heard the whine from the television tube warming up.

She stared at it, arms folded, waiting for the screen to come to life.

"I'd forgotten how long it takes for these stupid things to turn on," she muttered.

"I know what would improve our television experience," Rowan said brightly. "Some gadget that you could use to turn on the TV besides walking across the room and flicking the switch. I don't know, we could call it a . . . a . . . *remote* or something. What do you say? Wouldn't that be swell?"

"Yeah, that'd be really groovy," Kelly said equally brightly.

Snow came into focus.

Kelly turned the channel selector knob. There was snow on almost every channel. Only one had a badly distorted picture of what looked like farm equipment.

Kelly wrinkled her nose. "That sucks." She glanced at Rowan. Rowan looked as uneasy as she felt. She mustered a grin. "Well, bugger it. I didn't want to see cow commercials anyway." She turned off the television and picked up Rowan's cell phone from the desk. "No service. Not surprising."

"This is starting to creep me out," Rowan said.

Kelly sank down on the bed beside her. She pulled Rowan in close so Rowan's head was resting on her breasts. She stroked Rowan's back.

"We'll work through this somehow, sweetie," she said, marveling at the feel of Rowan's soft skin.

"That feels good," Rowan murmured. Her breathing evened out as she fell asleep.

Kelly lay awake for a long time beside her.

Rowan's right. This is really creepy. What the hell is going on? Where's Glen? I remember reading a story about a group of travelers in England who went back in time to the seventeenth century and when they fell asleep they came back again to our time. Is that what's going to happen to us here? Why *is this happening?*

Kelly's thoughts whirled and flew around inside her mind until she fell into a simple sleep of pure exhaustion.

ROWAN WOKE UP the next morning, immediately aware of two things. First, Kelly was still soundly asleep, nestled in her arms. Second, the television remote was resting on the bedside table next to the ringing alarm clock. She flicked it off.

Kelly began to stir. She kissed Rowan's chest and snuggled into her.

Rowan smiled. *She's so beautiful when she sleeps.* She pushed Kelly's hair back off her forehead. "Hey, sleepyhead. Time to get up."

"Don't wanna," Kelly mumbled. "Havin' a good dream."

"What would that be, love?" Rowan asked.

"Rowan kissed me."

"Rowan *did* kiss you. That was no dream."

Kelly's brown eyes slowly opened. "Oh yeah."

Rowan claimed her lips in a leisurely kiss, a promise of more to come.

"Do we have to leave?" Kelly asked plaintively when they broke. "Do we *have* to go to site?"

"Yes, we do." Rowan pulled her up so they were sitting up. "I want to be done today. I'm looking forward to our date tonight."

"And our day off tomorrow. We get to sleep in."

"Oh, hell, yes." Rowan watched her brown eyes darken with desire. "C'mon, we have to get moving so we can get this miserable day over and done with."

Kelly sighed and got off the bed, drawing Rowan with her. "All right. Just for you."

Rowan felt the tension flood back into Kelly's frame.

"It's better this morning, Kell. The TV is back the way it's supposed to be."

Kelly gritted her teeth and looked at the flat screen television. Her shoulders relaxed. "Thank God for that."

"I don't know what happened last night," Rowan said.

"I don't either and I think you're right. This scares the *shit* out of me."

"No matter what happens, we're together. That's the part that really matters. To me, at least."

Kelly squeezed Rowan tight. "It matters to me, too."

"I have to shower and change."

"Can I help?"

"I'd love for you to help but if you did we wouldn't get to site any time soon."

Kelly released Rowan. "I know." She openly took in Rowan's body from head to toes, gaze lingering on her breasts.

Rowan felt herself loosen inside and her nipples stiffened. "Kell."

"I know," Kelly said, sounding breathless. "I know. I'm going to get out of here." She shook her head and left.

Rowan sighed. Her body was throbbing unmercifully and her hands itched with the urge to tear of Kelly's clothes and take her.

She shook her head to clear it.

Half an hour later, there was a knock on the door just as she finished buttoning the last of her buttons on her blouse.

"Coming, Kell," she said, grabbing her suit coat from the back of her chair.

She pulled open the door and found Kelly standing outside, looking around the parking lot.

"What gives, Kell?" she asked, following the direction of her gaze. "Oh. Look at that."

The motel seemed longer and Kelly took Rowan's hand and pulled her into motion. As they passed the empty rooms, Rowan saw how *different* things looked in the light of day. The concrete was clean, as was the asphalt in the parking lot, new paint demarking the parking spaces. The rooms had new doors with magnetic locks. All the bay windows were one way so nothing inside was visible from the outside.

Kelly pulled her to a halt outside room twelve. "The curtains are open," she said, cupping her hands around her eyes and peering in. "I can see a suit bag, I think."

"So Glen's stuff *is* still here. Where's his car?" Rowan quickly surveyed the parking lot. The only car in it was theirs.

"He can't have gone far. He wouldn't leave his luggage behind."

"Call Rich. Tell him to keep trying Glen and to keep an eye out for him."

Kelly was already dialing her cell phone. "Done."

Rowan peered into the glass as Kelly spoke to Rich. The lights were off. The bed looked rumpled but not slept in. There was a lump on the bed that Rowan reasoned was his luggage. She couldn't see anything else through the reflective coating on the glass.

"Hey," Kelly said, breaking into her reverie. She was looking at her watch. "You want to grab some road breakfast? It's eight thirty."

"Good idea." Rowan turned from the room and surveyed the parking lot.

Everything seems normal this morning. What *is going on here?*

They went through the empty reception and into the back room that served as a breakfast room. Unlike the previous morning, one of the small tables had a group of four soldiers in fatigues sitting silently around it. They were devouring a hot breakfast and steadfastly not looking at each other.

Rowan and Kelly quickly grabbed some pastries and coffee and sat down.

"Interesting," Rowan said, leaning forward. "Guys in fatigues."

Kelly gave her a puzzled look. "Huh?"

Rowan smiled and felt uneasy. "Behind us. The table behind us."

"There's no one there. It's empty."

Rowan frowned. She turned and looked at the table. *It* is *empty. And there's no sign anyone was even* sitting *at it.* The chairs were pushed in and the table top was clean.

"Oh, hell," Rowan said. "I saw soldiers sitting at that table."

"It's starting again, isn't it?" Kelly said.

Rowan nodded. "Looks like it." She took a deep breath. "I want to finish at site today and get the hell out of here. I'm thinking overnight is when this weird thing that's going on is worse."

"Why do you say that?"

"Gut feel."

"Okay." Kelly stood. "Then let's get this squeaky show on the road so we can leave."

Rowan nodded.

The left the dining room and ten minutes later were at the stop sign that led down the brief stretch of road toward Department of Defense.

They pulled up into a parking spot, and Rowan grabbed Kelly's wrist as she was about to get out of the car.

Kelly gave her a questioning glance.

She stole a quick kiss. "Don't kill Ryan, okay? I'm not his, I'm yours."

Kelly smiled and caressed her face. "Okay."

"Let's get moving."

They got out of the car and walked into the building.

CHAPTER 8

"UGH." ROWAN PEERED at her laptop screen, Victor looking over her shoulder. "See this?" She tapped a graph on her screen. "See how high this is? That's not normal. Are you sure your network is fine?"

Victor nodded. "Pretty sure." He grinned. "But this is why we bought your software. To find out if things really were good."

Rowan studied the screen. *These errors are too high. I don't think it's a glitch. This doesn't fit any of the scenarios Glen found a couple of site visits ago.*

She glanced at Victor. "Could you please open up the system event log on the server?"

Victor moved his mouse to clear the screen saver and quickly typed in the password for the server. He opened the event log and Rowan looked quickly at it.

"Okay. I think we have it nailed. Looks like the network card on this machine is playing up." She smiled. "It's even kind enough to say that in the event log."

Victor returned her smile. "Yeah it does. I'm good with trying to swap it out. Okay, I'll just grab a spare from help desk and we can go down and change it."

I don't want to. "Sure," Rowan said.

"I'll be back in a tick," Victor said as he left.

Rowan sighed. *Yuck. That computer room sucks. But if Kelly can do this, so can I. Speaking of Kelly, wonder how she's doing?*

She looked out of the glass that was the front of Victor's office. He had his vertical blinds drawn back so he could see outside, he'd said. Rowan looked out at the sparsely peopled walkways, glad of the distraction.

There were soldiers standing around some locked doors, stone still and with an air of ever present vigilance. Civilians passed by them as though they were invisible. A flash of movement caught her eye. A cluster of four soldiers carefully escorted a civilian from a darkened side passage, past a pair of sentries, and into a locked door. They were heavily armed. They were gone quickly.

She replayed the scene over in her mind. *Huh?* She frowned. *Was that Glen? In handcuffs?*

She stood and stared at the door they'd gone through. *What the hell? Well, that would explain why we haven't found Glen. They have him for some reason.* She felt cold. *This is nuts.*

"Hey." Victor strode through the door, waving a network card around. "I'll just shut the machine down. Should be done by the time we get down there."

Rowan nodded. She studied the door.

"Are you all right?"

Rowan turned around. Victor had a wary expression on his face and studied her carefully.

"I'm fine." She pointed to the door. "What's behind the doors?" She smiled. "I'm not flipping out if that's what you're worried about."

"Oh. No. Not at all." Victor gave her a cautious smile. "Those doors lead to admin. You know, payroll, accounts and so on."

Rowan nodded. "Okay."

Victor still looked cautious and Rowan sighed internally. *David's probably going to hear about this. I'm sure Victor is going to tell Ryan I'm a loose cannon as well.*

"Let's go, shall we?" Rowan said. "The sooner we get this done the sooner we can finish fine tuning your monitoring."

Victor nodded. "All right."

They went to the lift, past unsmiling soldiers, and down to the basement computer room. The corridor was dark as the lift doors opened.

"How do you stand this?" Rowan said.

Victor smiled brightly. "Really well. That's why you see the computer room has so many people in it."

Rowan laughed as he swiped his badge against the card reader. He led the way to the rack mount and pulled out the computer. He lifted the lid and looked inside. "Damn."

"Oh," Rowan said. "Looks like we're going to need a different network card."

Victor nodded. "This card's too large. Give me a minute."

He was gone before Rowan could even acknowledge him.

She looked around as the lights turned off, one by one. *No wonder people feel uneasy down here.* She walked toward the end of the rack mount and an overhead light went on, bathing her in harsh, white light. *Better.* She saw something dark in her peripheral vision and quickly turned to zero in on it. Her heart rate sped up. She frowned as she looked down. A briefcase had caught her eye.

She hesitated a moment before she reached for it. She suppressed a fleeting sense of wrong doing as she pulled back the flap. *Notepad, pens, a repair kit, an Octahedron Software CD. This is* Glen's *briefcase.* She quickly rifled through the zippered compartments. Most of them were empty. One had a piece of paper in it—Glen's E-Ticket flight confirmation and his wallet.

That's not normal. At all. No one in their right mind would leave their wallet lying around like this. She quickly put it back and closed the briefcase. *That's coming with us.*

"Hey."

Rowan jumped at the sound of Victor's voice.

"Are you all right?" he asked. He looked concerned.

"I'm fine." Rowan patted the briefcase. "This is Glen's. I'm going to take it with me."

Victor nodded. "Sure." He gestured toward the server. "Shall we?"

Rowan nodded. "Let's."

"VERY GOOD." KELLY tossed a small chocolate to the woman who'd just answered her question. The woman caught it with a grin and unwrapped it with relish.

"Next question, and this one's for double points. Who can tell me where you configure another node?"

"Node administrator," one voice said.

"Almost."

"Server administrator."

"Right." Kelly tossed two chocolates. "Very good. You get to it through the command console." She looked at her watch. It was close to eleven. "Okay, everyone. Break time. I'll see everyone back here in ten minutes."

The room full of employees slowly stood. The low murmur of their voices came to her. Ryan waited for her at the back of the room.

"I must say," he said when they were alone. "I'm impressed. I had my doubts about Octahedron when Glen was here. But you and Rowan have done a marvelous job."

"Thank you." Kelly smiled. *Prick. You wish it was Rowan here, don't you?*

"Do you think you're going to be finished today?" he asked.

You better believe it. "I'm hoping so. We'd planned on staying in town until tomorrow, though, just in case you needed to call us back."

Ryan smiled in what looked like genuine pleasure. "That's wonderful. We appreciate that. Normally contractors take off as fast as they can. We're so out of the way." He folded his arms and smiled at her again. "I'd love to take the two of you out to dinner again this evening."

Kelly gritted her teeth. "Thank you, but I don't think we're going to be able to make it. We have some work issues that require our attention."

"Oh, that's a pity," he said.

"I'm sorry," Kelly said. *Ass.*

Ryan looked at his watch. "Break's almost over. I'm going to get some coffee. Can I get you something?"

"Yes, please. I'll take a coffee as well. White. Two sugars."

Ryan smiled. "White with two sugars. Got it. Back in a moment."

Kelly followed him out and headed toward the ladies toilet. As she was washing her hands, she heard a soft sob from one of the stalls. *Weird. No one was in here when I came in.*

She bent and looked under each of the doors. There were no feet anywhere to be seen and still the soft sobbing drifted to her.

"Hello? Does anyone need any help?"

Suddenly one of the doors flew open and she jumped back with a startled yelp. Her scalp crawled and the hair on her arms stood on end. A dark, translucent figure—a woman in fatigues—soundlessly strode out of the stall. She disappeared when she reached the sink.

Kelly never hesitated. She shot out of the toilet and strode down the corridor toward Victor's office. The skin between her shoulder blades itched and she had to stop herself from looking around. *She's gone. She disappeared, remember?*

She reached Victor's office. Rowan was sitting alone, studying her laptop.

She looked up when Kelly entered. "Hey, Kell," she said with a grin. The grin fell away. "What's the matter?"

Kelly stifled the urge to throw herself into Rowan's arms. "I'll fill you in later." She sat in the visitor's chair, folded her arms, and rested them on the desk. "How are you doing here? Are you on track to finish?"

Rowan smiled. "I should be asking you the same question. We're doing fine and yes, we'll be finished this afternoon." She leant forward, mirroring Kelly's posture. "I want to kiss you."

Kelly caught a flash of Rowan's full breasts. "I want you to kiss me."

Rowan shook her head. She snorted a laugh and looked frustrated. "I don't know how I'm going to get through today. I want you."

"Focus and get this job done," Kelly said. "And then you can have me. In fact, I'd appreciate it if you did."

Rowan laughed softly. "Are you going to be able to make lunch?"

Kelly nodded. "Of course."

"Good. Then let's do lunch."

"You're on." She looked at Rowan's watch. "Eleven ten. Break time's over." She stood to leave.

"Kell."

Kelly turned around. Her throat went dry at the sight of

Rowan, leaning back in her chair. Her blouse was slightly open and Kelly had to drag her eyes away from the cleft of Rowan's breasts. "Yes, boss?"

"Come and get me when you leave for lunch."

"You're on."

"YOU READY?"

Rowan looked up at Kelly, leaning comfortably in the doorway.

"I'm ready," she said, standing and stretching. Kelly watched her appreciatively.

"Where's Victor?" Kelly asked.

"He's in a meeting with Ryan. I think they're giving us a performance review."

They headed down the stairs toward the cafeteria.

Rowan leaned in closer to Kelly, breathing in the gentle scent of her perfume. "You smell nice," she said softly. "I've always thought that."

"I always thought the same thing about you," Kelly said equally softly.

They entered the cafeteria and chose their food—salads for both. Rowan paid and led them to a corner table at the edge of the room. The tables around them were empty.

"You want to tell me what happened to you this morning? You were as white as a sheet," Rowan said.

"I'll tell you at dinner this evening," Kelly said. "I'm not really comfortable talking here."

Rowan studied at her. Kelly looked pale and strained. *I really want to take her hand but I can't.* "All right, I can live with that." She took another bite of her salad. "I've got something to tell you as well but it'll wait."

Kelly looked at her. "Nothing bad, I hope."

"No, of course not," Rowan said. "I have to tell you something now, though. I found Glen's briefcase."

"Really?" Kelly said. "Where?"

"Down in the computer room. Leaning against the end tower of the server racks."

Kelly frowned. "I didn't see it there yesterday and trust me, I looked around pretty carefully before ... you know. Do you think someone put it there to throw us off?"

Rowan remembered Glen being escorted by soldiers. "That's a possibility."

Kelly looked as though she wanted to say something, but instead shook her head and kept eating her salad.

When they finished, Kelly escorted Rowan back up to Victor's office. Victor was waiting for her with a broad smile.

"You ready?" he asked.

"Catch you later," Kelly whispered into Rowan's ear, squeezing her arm as she left.

Rowan's skin tingled from her gentle touch. She cleared her throat. "I'm ready."

CHAPTER 9

ROWAN KNOCKED ON Kelly's door and waited. The door opened and Kelly immediately pulled her inside. Kelly's arms slipped around her and they kissed.

"Good to see you, too," Rowan said when they broke.

"I've wanted to do that all day," Kelly said, running her fingers along the sides of Rowan's breasts. "You look terrific."

"So do you. I'm only wearing jeans."

"You won't be for long."

Rowan smiled. "Are you hungry?"

"Starved, actually. On both fronts."

"I promised you a real date." Rowan stroked Kelly's face. "And I'd like to deliver no matter how grumpy my body is about it."

Kelly laughed and leant into her touch. "I hear you. We'd better go before we can't leave."

Rowan took her hand and they went to the car. They got in and headed toward the T intersection. Kelly's hand rested comfortably on Rowan's thigh.

Rowan gestured toward the sign when they got there. "Which shall it be? Ithaca or Settler's Creek?"

Kelly was silent for a moment. "Why don't we try Ithaca? We're less likely to run into Ryan or Victor."

"Ithaca it is, then."

Rowan put out her indicator and turned left. The fresh asphalt petered out quickly. Unlike the road to Settler's Creek which was well paved, this one was more a series of potholes held together by asphalt as an afterthought.

"This is weird," Rowan said as they wound their way down the other side of the ridge.

"Yeah." Kelly looked all around them. "Ithaca doesn't exist anymore, does it? I figured they rebuilt it after the fire."

"So did I," Rowan said.

They pulled up into a sandy parking lot, in front of a sign that said *Ithaca Memorial Village.*

"This is no village," Kelly said.

Rowan stopped the engine, and they got out of the car. Behind the chained-off dirt road was a series of ruins. Most of the ruins were of old buildings and what looked like a house or two. It had been reclaimed by the bush and they heard insects and birds rustling in the leaves. A fresh breeze filtered through the trees, increasing the hissing sound from the moving leaves and bathing them in cold air.

"This is creepy." Rowan looked at Kelly. "I'm starting to get bored with using *creepy* and *weird* to describe this place."

"Those words fit the best, though."

"They do." Rowan caught a flash of movement out of the corner of her eye and turned to follow it. "What's that?"

Kelly shifted and looked in the same direction. "That looks like a man."

"Oh, my. Yes, it does."

A translucent man stood in the middle of what was once the main street of Ithaca. He stared straight ahead and wore dirty, shapeless pants, a dusty shirt, and a worn hat.

Rowan moved toward him, only dimly aware of Kelly's protestations.

He remained still and apparently oblivious of Rowan's presence. She could see his stubbly face and dark eyes.

She caught more movement out of the corner of her eye and turned to track it. All around her, slowly and surely, a country bush town sprang into being.

"Kell, you have to see this." She waved her arm toward Kelly as women in long dresses floated an inch or two above the ground. They went into ruined buildings, opening doors that weren't there and vanishing once they went through them.

She was distantly aware of Kelly's proximity as two men on horses made their way down the street in eerie silence. Children played, men and women walked, and dogs barked, all silent and unaware.

"Holy fuck," Kelly said softly.

"I know," Rowan said.

"Let's back it up and get out of here," Kelly said.

Rowan turned at the urgency in her tone. "What gives, Kell?"

Kelly tugged Rowan into motion and they went back to the car. "There's something badly wrong here, Rowan."

"You're afraid of ghosts?"

"I'm not sure we're dealing with ghosts," Kelly said.

They crossed over the chain barrier. Rowan turned back to the ruins and frowned. "It's empty again."

"I figured," Kelly said. "Let's go to Settler's Creek."

Rowan caught Kelly's sense of urgency and quickly turned the car around and began the bumpy drive back up to the top of the ridge.

"If you don't think that was ghosts, what do you think it was?" Rowan asked as they went through the stop sign and back down the ridge toward Settler's Creek.

"I'll tell you over dinner. I'm still trying to work it out in my head."

They went to the outskirts of town and Rowan stopped at another stop sign. Instead of going straight in to the town, they turned left and travelled for a few minutes along the outskirts.

"Where are we going?" Kelly asked.

"Surprise destination. Yesterday when we went to dinner, I noticed we went past a sign that pointed to Skyline Restaurant. I thought we'd try that."

"I like it." Kelly squeezed Rowan's thigh.

Rowan caressed her hand, then drew it up and kissed her knuckles. "I hope you're not tired."

"I'm not," Kelly said softy. "On edge but *not* tired. Not when you're around."

"Here we are," Rowan said as they pulled into the parking lot of a restaurant on the edge of a plain. There was a breathtaking view of the ridge in the distance.

"This is incredible," Kelly said.

"Yeah, it is. Wonder if they have seating outside?"

"I hope so."

They went into the restaurant. It was the size of a ballroom with a giant aquarium filled with tropical fish. On one wall was a mural of a beach scene. The other walls were filled with nautical memorabilia—sextants, spoked wheels, paintings of nautical scenes, fishing nets, and a dory suspended from the ceiling.

"Wow," Kelly said.

Rowan nodded.

"Table for two?" a woman asked from behind them.

Rowan started.

"I'm sorry," the woman continued as Rowan turned toward her. She was middle aged with dyed, dark hair and a new, clean dress. "I didn't mean to scare you."

"No worries," Rowan said with an easy smile. "Yes, please. A table for two. Outside, if you have one."

"Certainly we do. Follow me."

They trailed behind her to the floor-to-ceiling bay windows. There was a door one side and she held it open for them.

Rowan followed behind Kelly, eyes glued to her beautiful form, as she chose a seat on the edge of the patio.

They sat and the woman handed them both menus.

"What's your special?" Rowan asked.

"Gnocchi Neopolitana," the woman said.

"That sounds good. I'll have that," Rowan said.

Kelly glanced at her. "Same."

"Drinks?"

"Just water for me," Rowan said.

"Same," Kelly said.

"We have a lot to talk about," Kelly said, dragging her gaze from Rowan's breasts to her face.

Rowan's nipples tightened. "Oh, hell. You *have* to stop looking at me like that in public. It's killing me to be this close to you and not be able to touch you."

Kelly nodded. "I know. The world sucks, doesn't it? I wish I could be all over you in public like straight people."

"When we get home," Rowan said.

"Can't wait for that," Kelly said with a marked lack of enthusiasm.

"Ah. Genevieve."

"I'm not looking forward to that."

"I know, but I'll be there with you if you want me to be."

Kelly looked shyly surprised and pleased. "I'll think about it. Definitely."

"I know we have to talk about us," Rowan said.

Their drinks arrived and Rowan waited until the woman walked away.

"I was gonna say, I know we have to talk about us and we will. But I need to talk about today," she continued.

"So do I," Kelly said. "What happened to you today?"

"I went down to the computer room and found Glen's briefcase. You know that. But before we went down, while I was waiting for Victor to come back with a new network card, I think I saw Glen."

"You *what?*"

"I think I saw Glen. He was being escorted to a room by a group of soldiers."

Kelly looked annoyed. "Why didn't you tell me?"

"I don't know how real it was," Rowan said. "I asked Vic what was behind the door and he said it was admin—payroll, accounting, and so on. I've been seeing things ever since we got here. I've been seeing soldiers all over the building and they *never* pay attention to anyone. No one pays attention to them. Are they even really there?"

Kelly frowned. "That part makes sense at least. But what about Glen?"

"Why on earth would a bunch of soldiers be taking Glen into admin offices?"

"That's if they *were* admin offices."

"Why are soldiers standing outside the offices? There are two possibilities. Victor was lying and those *weren't* admin offices. Or the soldiers and Glen weren't really there."

"What in God's name is going on here?"

"I don't know."

"You think it's some kind of weird temporal or spatial distortion?" Kelly blushed.

"You're very beautiful when you blush. And yes, that's what I'm starting to think. Think about it. The motel room's television set changing. Reception changing. The missing room twelve."

Kelly was silent for a moment, mulling it over. "Yeah, that *does* make sense, which is scary. It would also explain the toilet and woman in fatigues."

"Pardon me?"

"Oh. Yeah. I wanted to tell you. I saw a soldier today that scared the shit out of me. I went into the toilet, and I heard a woman crying. I checked the stalls and I was alone in there. Suddenly one of the doors flew open and a female soldier came out. She disappeared when she got to the sink."

"Oh, Sweetie, is that why you looked so spun out when you saw me this morning?"

"Yes."

Their food arrived. Rowan smiled her thanks at the woman. She gave them a disgusted look. Rowan shrugged as soon as her back was turned.

"I think she worked out we're bent."

"Fuck her."

"Agreed."

They were silent for a minute.

"There's a big part of me that just wants to get the hell out of here," Kelly said. "If we are dealing with something like a spatial distortion, how do we know *we* can get out of here?"

Good question. "How do we know we're not already in it?"

"We don't. If last night is anything to go by then I think things kick up overnight."

"So if we ride out the oddness tonight, we should end up back here again tomorrow morning."

Kelly nodded. "We know that all of this starts here. As soon as we leave here my gut tells me that we're going to stay in whatever world was here when we left. So if we go through a rift tonight and leave we get stuck in the rift."

Rowan nodded. "It's possible. It's as good an idea as any

other." She grinned at Kelly. "I can't say my education covered how to deal with spatial rifts."

Kelly laughed with her.

The other reason we can't leave is because it's starting again. "Kell, look." Rowan inclined her head toward the restaurant. The artificial light inside was a harsh contrast to the late twilight outside. The mural on the wall had changed from a beach scene to a mountain.

Kelly looked dismayed. "Oh, no."

I don't care who sees us. Rowan took her hand. "Relax, sweetie. This has happened to us twice so far. Both times we came back to where we were supposed to be. There's no reason to believe that we won't end up back in our time and place tomorrow morning. Either possibility is equally likely."

"I know you're right," Kelly said. "But now that I have a good clue what's going on, I'm more scared than ever."

"Whatever happens, we're together. I'm right beside you for the whole thing."

Kelly squeezed her hand. "That makes me feel a little better. Thank you."

"What's that?" Rowan looked up at the ridgeline and it looked as though a searchlight beamed up into the night sky.

"I don't know," Kelly said. "I think it's coming from the fire pit."

I have to go up there. I have to see this.

Kelly looked at her. "I want to see." It was as though she'd read Rowan's mind.

"I'm in." Rowan stood and pushed her chair back. Kelly quickly followed suit and them—she now wore a name tag that said *Esther*—glared at them as they approached.

"You're disgusting," she said before either of them could speak. "You should be locked up and executed. Leave now or I'm calling the police."

Rowan's temper sparked. She drew herself up to her full height and stared down at the woman. "I'd love to accommodate you. However, I need to pay the bill first. How about you give that to me?"

The woman thrust a small slip of paper at her. "You're going to burn in hell."

"You bring the chips, I'll bring the dip," Rowan said coldly, tossing her credit card toward the woman.

"Couldn't find a man?" she continued as the woman positioned the slip and credit card and viciously dragged the handle back and forth to get a credit card impression. "Is that why you're unnatural? Trying to rebel? You need to be raped so you know what it's for."

God what a horrible thing to say to someone.

"No, actually," Kelly piped up before Rowan could fully unleash her temper. "We're just trying to leave and escape your boring monologue, you vicious bigot."

Rowan put her credit card back into her wallet as the woman thrust the slip in her direction to sign. Rowan signed and the woman made a production of tossing the pen into a garbage can behind the counter.

"Freak. Get out." She pointed at the door.

Rowan smiled. "With pleasure, cutie."

"Get out," the woman screamed. Her eyes flashed with rage.

Rowan felt as though she'd been hit with low grade poison gas.

They left the restaurant.

"Wow, what a homophobe." Rowan looked around the parking lot. It looked as retro as the motel looked. There were some ancient cars in immaculate condition in the parking lot, and the one or two lone diners were dressed as though they'd just walked out of the fifties. "Look at this."

"I know, this is weird. There's that word again. Damn." Kelly slipped her hand into Rowan's. "We have to get out of here. She's on the phone."

Rowan glanced back at the woman as she spoke into the receiver. Both of her hands curled around the plastic in what Rowan supposed was a white knuckled grip. The woman kept glancing at them as though burned. She still looked angry.

"Okay," Rowan said.

They got into the car and left the parking lot.

Rowan glanced around, looking for police cars. So far, there weren't any. All the cars they passed looked the same as the ones parked at the restaurant. They made the turn onto to the road leading back up the ridge. Rowan glanced in the rearview mirror just as they rounded the first hairpin bend. A police car drifted through the stop sign.

"Did you just see the police car?" Kelly asked.

"Yep. I'm amazed. I didn't think she was serious."

Kelly shivered. "Let's just get out of here."

Rowan nodded. "Agreed."

Kelly kept watch out of the back window as they went up the hill. There was no sign of the police.

Rowan made the turn at the T intersection at the top of the hill. They headed toward the fire pit and she felt herself relaxing. She hadn't realized she was so tense. Kelly caressed Rowan's thigh and her body began throbbing.

"God, what weird night," she said.

"I know," Kelly said. "I just want to be alone with you. Fuck the world."

Rowan smiled and she felt it and her relaxation fade away. "What the fuck is this?"

CHAPTER 10

"OH MY GOD," Kelly said. "What the fuck?"

Rowan slowly drove past the place that had been Department of Defense during the day.

It was still a huge office building but it looked less modern and airy and more utilitarian. It bristled with menace. Ten foot barbed wire fences surrounded the property. A boom gate with armed soldiers marked what had been the entrance to the parking lot. The soldiers eyed them as they drove past and Rowan sped up, unwilling to draw more of their attention.

"This doesn't look good. Now we know for sure this isn't a silly ghost story," Rowan said. "I don't know where we are but we aren't in Kansas anymore, Dorothy."

Kelly shook her head. "No. We're not."

They pulled into the parking lot by the fire pit and Rowan stopped the car. They eyed a column of wispy, eerie light that shone up into the heavens like a visitor from another world.

"Come on," Rowan said, getting out of the car.

Kelly caught her wrist. "Are you sure this is such a good idea?"

"How can this get worse? We're not in our own world anymore, and to make it more interesting, the world we landed in runs on homophobia."

"All the more reason to get the hell out of here."

"I won't argue with you on that one. If the same pattern from the last few nights still holds, when we wake up tomorrow we should be back where we belong. So don't worry about that part." Rowan pulled Kelly into motion and they walked toward the light.

Rowan felt as though she was being blasted by x rays. The light shone through her body and when she held up her hands she could see her bones outlined in muscle and skin. Yet the light wasn't blinding her.

She waved her hand. It was like it was a series of still frames. She saw many versions of her hand before her eyes.

"I don't like this at all," she said. Her voice sounded slurred and she felt the first stirring of real fear.

"Can we get out of here, please?" Kelly sounded as muddy as Rowan did.

Rowan nodded—it felt like her neck had a brace on it—and they went back to the car. It was like walking through thick mud. She felt exhausted and was dripping with sweat as they got into the car.

She started the car and they left the parking lot. She glanced at Kelly, was as white as a sheet and her face and neck glistened with sweat.

Rowan felt better as they drove away from the godforsaken fire pit. Kelly looked more relaxed as well.

They pulled into the parking lot of the motel. It was as empty of cars as it had been for most of their stay there.

Rowan got out. She smiled at Kelly. "Are you coming?"

"I don't want to be alone." Kelly slipped her hand into Rowan's and Rowan unlocked the door to her room with a large, brass key.

She opened the door and let Kelly in. She tossed the key onto the desk with a snort, suppressing her uneasiness.

She reached toward the light switch but felt Kelly's hand gently take hers.

"I don't want to be alone tonight." Kelly teased her tank top free from her jeans.

Rowan's need took over and she kissed Kelly hard. Her breath caught as Kelly broke the kiss and pulled her tank top over her head. Her bra swiftly followed and Kelly kissed the slope of her breasts, down to her nipples. She sucked Rowan's nipple gently into her mouth and nipped it.

Rowan moaned, catching her fingers in Kelly's hair.

"Just you and me. Forget the world," Rowan whispered,

drawing Kelly up and unbuttoning her jeans. She kissed Kelly and felt her bare skin under her fingertips.

Rowan was dimly aware that somehow they'd collapsed onto the bed together and that Kelly was straddling her. Her mind fled and instinct took over as Kelly kissed her way down Rowan's body. She came almost as soon as Kelly entered her, crying out her orgasm.

She reciprocated, enjoying every inch of Kelly's skin, finding the places that made her sigh, and the ones that made her hot and breathless.

They began again almost as soon as they finished. They finally fell asleep in the early hours of the morning, tangled together, with the sheets pooled around their waists.

KELLY WOKE UP the next morning, half lying on Rowan. Rowan's arm was around her, holding her close. Her beautiful face, at close range, was still relaxed in sleep.

Last night was fantastic. She's so gentle and passionate. I want to build something with her, if she'll have me. It won't be easy but I'm willing to try. I hope she wants the same thing. I hope she feels the same. I'd do anything for her. I admit it. I'm crazy in love with her.

She gently disentangled herself from Rowan's grip and rested on her elbows, studying her striking face. Rowan's beautiful, cornflower blue eyes opened and her lips curved into a smile.

"Hi," she said softly.

Kelly kissed her. "Hi."

"Are you okay with last night?"

"Very much so. You?" *I love you.*

"Yes." Rowan ran her fingertips down the side of Kelly's face. "God, you're so beautiful."

"You really think so?"

"No. I'm lying to you."

Kelly laughed. "Thank you, then."

Rowan's gaze fastened to a point over her shoulder and her eyes widened. She stiffened and sat up. "Oh, no."

"What?" Kelly asked, alarmed.

Rowan kept staring over her shoulder.

Kelly frowned and turned around. "Shit. Oh, shit."

The motel room looked like a wreck. The television was gone and the walls were filthy and covered in cobwebs. The wallpaper was peeling off the walls in places. The mattress they lay on was covered in moldering sheets. Kelly quickly got out of bed, pulling Rowan with her.

"Oh, no," Rowan said. "We didn't end up in our reality, did we?"

Kelly shook her head. "Nope, doesn't look like it."

Rowan grabbed her watch. She grimaced at the dusty smear on her fingers. "It's the day after yesterday's site visit. I know we're displaced but wherever we are, it's the same date."

Kelly began pulling on her clothes, Rowan immediately following suit. She went into the bathroom—as dusty and empty as the rest of the motel room—and turned the tap handle. It screeched and remained dry. She opened the toilet lid. It was bone dry.

No smell. The pipes have been dry for a while.

"This is bad," Rowan said from behind her.

Kelly jumped. She turned and slipped into Rowan's arms, loving the solid feel of her body.

"Yeah, this is bad," Kelly said. "I'm trying not to panic."

"Don't panic, sweetie. The only thing we can do is just deal with this."

Kelly's temper sparked. She pulled back. "*Deal* with this? *I* wanted to leave. I wanted to get the hell out of here yesterday. *You* wanted to stay."

Rowan glared at her. "Are you blaming *me* for this?"

"We're still here because of you."

Rowan's shoulders slumped. "I'm sorry, Kell." She threw up her hands and left the bathroom. A second or so later Kelly heard Rowan throw her duffel bag on the bed and the sound of the zipper.

Kelly sighed and grabbed the edges of the sink. She looked at her face in the flyspecked mirror. Her eyes were red and tears leaked from them.

Oh, shit. Why am I mad at Rowan? If I'd wanted us to leave I could have pushed harder. I'm just as responsible for this as she is. She closed her eyes. She felt forlorn and miserable.

She felt arms encircle her and pull her in close. She felt Rowan kiss the side of her neck.

"I'm so sorry, Kell. I didn't mean to drag you into this mess with me. You're right. We *should* have left yesterday."

Kelly shifted in her arms, pressing her face against the side of Rowan's neck. "I'm sorry, love. I don't mean to be mad at you. I'm just tense and I took it out on you."

"It's okay, Kell. I understand."

Rowan held her, gently soothing her tears. After a while she drew back. "We can't stay here. This motel is a wreck."

"I know," Kelly said. "What if we were to ride out today, stay here and see what happens? How do we know things won't snap back tonight?"

Rowan sighed. "Sounds like a good idea. Let's go into Settler's Creek and see if there's somewhere else to stay?"

Kelly nodded. "That's as good an idea as any."

Rowan took her hand and led her back to the bed. She rubbed her hands up and down Kelly's arms. "You're freezing."

"I'm cold," Kelly said. "It's *cold* in here." *This is a lot colder than our motel is. It's the same time of year, so it should be summer. This can't be right.* "I'm going to go back to my room and grab a tee shirt."

Rowan nodded. She dug in her bag and pulled out a polo shirt.

Kelly slipped out of the room and looked around. The car was parked on ancient and crumbling asphalt. Weeds sprang up through the cracks, growing all the way up to the car's wheel well. The motel sign was faded and broken. The rest of the motel itself was a derelict shell of its former self. Half of the windows were broken, some of them covered with plywood that was half rotten and water stained. The glass surrounding reception was dull and filthy.

Oh, no.

Kelly went to her room. The door was shut. She searched her

pockets quickly for a key and found none. She twisted the door knob. She was sure the door would be locked. It turned easily in her hand. She opened it.

Oh, hell no.

The room looked like it hadn't been used for years. An ancient and moldering bed sat by one wall, covered in a mattress that was half rotten and water stained. The desk, bedside table and wardrobe, were bare.

My stuff isn't here. What does that mean?

"Where's your stuff?" Rowan asked from behind her.

"I don't know." Kelly turned to Rowan, heart hammering with dread. "This isn't good, is it?"

"I don't know what this means," Rowan said. "I don't know what *any* of this means. Come with me. You can borrow some of my stuff."

Kelly nodded dumbly and followed Rowan out of the room. She felt almost numb.

"Look at this." Rowan held up her cell phone.

"Your cell phone. What about it?"

"Look who the carrier is," Rowan said.

Kelly read the screen. It said *Telecom.* "Shouldn't that be Telstra?"

Rowan nodded. "It should."

"I'm going to say the words, no matter how stupid they sound. We're not in our reality anymore, are we?" She felt her face heat.

Rowan bit her lip. "No, I don't think we are either." She reached into her back pocket and pulled out a folded piece of paper. "There's more. Check this out."

Kelly unfolded the piece of paper and read it. It was an invoice for a place called *The Ithaca Hotel.* The stay was for three nights.

"You stayed in Ithaca?"

"Looks like," Rowan said.

Kelly sat down on the bed, pulling Rowan with her. She fought down a rising sense of fear. "I'm scared, Rowan, but this isn't the time for brain lock." She took Rowan's hand. "It's the same as it's been for the past few days. It's you and me. Together. I think we can work through whatever weird shit is going on here. There are two choices we have, here. First, we can stay another night and hope that we snap back into our reality. Second, we can disappear into this reality and just go back down to Sydney. We can see if Glen is here."

"Very astute," Rowan said after a minute. "Option one is the most sensible thing to do."

"I think so as well," Kelly said, glad Rowan had opted for their first choice. Her low grade sense of disquiet came to the fore and she pushed it back. "I don't want to stay in this motel tonight. Let's go down to Ithaca and see if we can get a night at the hotel you just stayed at." She shivered.

"Oh, here," Rowan said. She grabbed a polo shirt that had been resting on top of her duffel bag and waited for Kelly to pull it on. "Better?"

Kelly nodded.

"Good." Rowan pulled her in close and kissed her temple. "I agree with you. We should go down to Ithaca and get another night at that hotel. If we're lucky we'll wake up early tomorrow morning in a ghost town."

"That sounds strangely appealing," Kelly said and they laughed. It felt good. Some of the shadows withdrew.

"Let's get moving," Rowan said. "I don't know about you but I'm hungry and I need a shower."

"And a toilet," Kelly said.

Rowan laughed. "Yeah, that'd be nice."

Rowan grabbed her luggage and they left the motel room.

It was full daylight outside, and the light had a sickening, greenish twinge to it.

What's that smell?

The smell was like an undertone of rotting meat. The scent of warm eucalyptus was gone. It was *cold*. Kelly could see the breath frosting in front of her face.

"It's March. It should be warm but it's *freezing* out here." Kelly shivered.

Rowan immediately drew her in close. "I know. I don't like this."

"Look at the sky." The sky had a greenish tinge and was troubling to look at. She could only glance up for a few seconds and then she had to look away. She felt a deep seated uneasiness.

She looked at the untamed bush that bordered the ruined motel. It had a sickly yellow tinge. She felt Rowan slip her hand into hers.

"This doesn't look good at all." Rowan's soft voice sounded like a gunshot in the quiet stillness.

Kelly nodded. "No, it doesn't." She looked around the edges of the motel. "Hah. Look at that." She nodded toward the end rooms. "There's a room twelve, I think."

"Let's take a quick look," Rowan said, pulling her into motion.

They walked across the parking lot and Kelly felt grateful for Rowan's proximity.

They peered into the room, but couldn't see much through the dirty glass. The door was slightly ajar and Kelly pushed it open so they could go in.

She blinked, her eyes adjusting to the lower light level.

"Look at that," Rowan said.

Kelly looked at the bed.

It was a bare mattress with a layer of dust on it. Some of the dust was gone, making it look as though it'd been slept in recently.

Does that mean Glen was here?

She exchanged a look with Rowan and saw from the faint frown furrowing her smooth forehead that the same thought had occurred to Rowan.

"What's that?" Rowan said.

Kelly followed the direction of her gaze.

Something was half visible under the side of the bed. Kelly bent down to look at it.

It was a magnetic key to a motel room. It looked the same as the ones that they'd gotten when they'd checked into the motel. Kelly got onto her knees and peered under the bed. She reached out and tugged a pile of rags toward her.

Those aren't rags.

"That's a set of fatigues, isn't it?" Rowan bent over with her hands on her knees.

Kelly nodded. She pulled the tee shirt out so it was straight and saw that it was covered in dirt and a splash of blood.

Rowan picked up the pants and rifled through the pockets. She dug into one of them and pulled out a cell phone. She sat down on the edge of the bed, Kelly beside her, and turned it on.

As soon as it powered up, it flashed a low battery alarm and Rowan quickly went into the contacts list and scanned it.

"There's our numbers. They're the right numbers," she said, viewing the detail on the *Rowan* and *Boss Lady* entries. She looked at Kelly as the phone beeped and powered down. "This is really Glen's phone."

Kelly nodded. "Okay, what do you want to do now?"

Rowan sighed and was quiet for a few moments. "We have a couple of choices. We can stay here and see if we snap back to our reality overnight. Or we can try and find Glen."

"We don't know if Glen is actually here. We know his *cell phone* is here."

"You saw a guy in the computer room who was in fatigues. We're in a different world to the one we went to sleep in last night, which was different to the one we woke up in yesterday morning. You want to know what I *really* think?"

"I don't think you have to try and tell me. I think I know where you're going with this. We're changing realities, aren't we?"

Rowan nodded.

"Glen could be in any one of the worlds we've seen so far. Where does the guy in fatigues fit into all of this?"

"We could try to find him so we could ask?"

Kelly gaped at her. "You're kidding, right?"

Rowan shook her head. "What do you want to do?"

There's more than one thing I want to know. I want to know how and why we're world hopping. I want to know who the guy in fatigues is. I want to know where Glen is.

"I think we should stay here tonight. I'd like to get home. I don't feel good here. If we don't world hop, then we find the person who was wearing the fatigues so we can ask what's going on here."

Rowan nodded after a moment. "Agreed." She stood and held out her hand. "Let's get a room for the night."

"Sounds like a good idea to me."

CHAPTER 11

ROWAN STOPPED AT the stop sign. The road was in ill repair although it looked used. The familiar three way sign was there. Right led to Settler's Creek, left to Ithaca, and straight ahead was the most troubling of all. The faded green road sign said *Department of Catastrophe and Climate Change.*

"Go straight ahead," Kelly said.

Rowan agreed. *This makes me feel sick.*

They drifted through the stop sign. The road ahead was in the same state of disrepair as the others. *Those gum trees. Oh my God. They make me sick to look at them. They're almost dead.*

They pulled up at the edge of a parking lot. The building ahead was old and ill kept. It was about half the size of the modern building they'd spent the last couple of days in. It looked like it'd been built sometime in the fifties and hadn't been touched since then. The steel frames on the small, dirty windows were heavily oxidized. Trails of rust ran down the sides of the building from them. There weren't many cars in the parking lot and those that were looked no newer than about ten years old. The entire air was one of neglect and desolation.

"I've seen enough," Kelly said quietly, breaking Rowan out of her reverie. "Let's go down to Ithaca."

Rowan did a neat U turn and they went back to the stop sign. They headed down the road toward Ithaca.

A few minutes later, they'd made it to where the parking lot to the ruined town had been. The parking lot was gone, replaced by a desultory sign marking the edge of the town of Ithaca. The paint was peeling from it and the jaunty, cheerful signage of *Welcome to Ithaca* was almost illegible. A wide street was ahead of them, the paving ill kept and the curbs crumbling in places.

The first few houses they passed looked empty and *for sale* signs leant at drunken angles in front of some of them.

The commercial district had an even mix of empty and open shops. There was a supermarket, an op shop, a real estate agent and a desultory police station.

We haven't seen anyone and there are barely any cars on the streets. Even the police station seems vacant. They reached another T intersection and Rowan turned left, following a sign that said *Ithaca Hotel.*

A moment or so later they pulled up outside what looked like a pub. They got out.

The doors to the pub were open and they could hear the sound of a television in the distance.

"Ready?" Rowan asked as she pulled her duffel out of the back of the car.

Kelly nodded.

Rowan took her hand and they went into the pub. It was almost empty. A couple of men in dusty clothing sat at a table near to the television. The weather channel was on and blaring, but Rowan couldn't distinguish individual words.

The bar itself was empty and they went past it, following a small sign that said *Hotel Reception.* Kelly pushed open the door and they found themselves in what looked like a normal hotel reception, with a small concierge desk, a reception desk, and the hotel porter desk.

"Look at the desks," Rowan said softly.

They were all long disused, except for reception. That was the only one not covered in a thick layer of dust and air of desolation.

The door to the office behind reception was open and Rowan could hear someone moving around. Kelly smartly hit the bell on top of the desk—*ring for service*—and a middle aged man immediately came out.

His eyes lit up when he saw Rowan, and narrowed in disapproval when he saw Kelly.

Here we go again. Rowan rolled internal eyes. *I'm getting tired of being ticketed by the homo police.*

"Hello, love," he said. "Help you? Did you leave something behind?"

"I'd like another room for the night."

"You can have the same room. All right." He jabbed his chin toward Kelly. "What about her?" He frowned. "You know our policy on single people in this hotel. No sinful behavior."

Rowan bit her lip to contain a snort of laughter. She struggled to remain expressionless.

"There's no hanky panky going on here," Kelly said smoothly, with a winning smile. "I'm perfectly prepared to keep my hands to myself."

He eyed them both severely. "See to it. No fornication out of wedlock."

Rowan bit her lip harder. She handed the clerk her credit card and he swiped it.

She signed in and accepted a brass key thrust in her direction. Kelly followed suit.

Rowan grabbed her luggage and they went to the stairs on the far wall. After two flights of creaky stairs they were headed down the hallway toward their rooms.

Rowan had just let herself into her room and dropped her duffel onto the neatly made bed when her cell phone rang.

Caller ID said it was *David*.

"Morning, David," she said. "How are you this fine morning?"

"Good, Rowan, yourself?" David's cheerful, disembodied voice asked. "How'd you make out at Climate Change?"

"Install went well. I'll be in the office on Monday morning."

"*Install went well?*" David snorted. "That's an understatement. They loved you." Rowan could hear the smile in his voice. "Good. Have a safe trip back. How long's the drive?"

Rowan frowned. *Drive?* "Twenty-four hours plus. With stops, of course."

David laughed. "Be safe. Take it easy. We'll see you on Monday."

"No worries. See you then."

Rowan hung up the phone. Kelly had come during the call and gave her a questioning look.

"Was that David?" Kelly asked.

"Yep. I don't have to be in the office until Monday, which is nice."

"Did he ask about me at all?"

"No," Rowan said. "I don't like this. It's like you don't exist."

"That's what I thought." Kelly sat down on the bed. "I checked my wallet. My driver's license is the same one I brought with me on this trip. I don't have any luggage. Where am I in this world?"

"You could be down in Sydney somewhere. Don't read anything bad into this."

"Easy for you to say," Kelly said. "You're here. You've got a job and a life. I'm starting to think I don't have any of that."

"Even if you don't, Kell, you still have me. Stay with me. *Be* with me."

Something flickered in Kelly's dark eyes. She put her hand on Rowan's cheek and drew her close for a gentle kiss. Rowan felt her toes curling as the kiss deepened. When it finished, Rowan was glad she was sitting down. Her knees felt wobbly and a barrage of emotion hammered her from all sides.

I'm in so much trouble with her. I think I'm in love. Oh, no. I'm sure she doesn't want that.

"Wow," she said. She sounded as shaky as she felt. "Where did you learn to do that?"

"There's just something about you," Kelly said. "It's *you.*"

She looked vulnerable and slightly afraid. Rowan pulled her in close, laid her cheek on Kelly's head, and rocked her back and forth slightly. "Never worry, Kelly. I'm here. I'm always going to be right here."

Kelly pulled back and gave her a searching gaze. "Are you saying what I think you're saying?"

"What do you think I'm saying?" Rowan whispered. *I'm such a chickenshit.*

"I think you're telling me you're more than just attracted to me, aren't you?"

Rowan hesitantly nodded.

"Good." Kelly kissed her again. "I'm more than just attracted to you as well." Kelly pulled her close and held her hard. "I love you, Rowan May."

Rowan felt like she wanted to jump for joy. "I love you too, Kelly Carne. So much." She shook with the relief that flooded through her like a tidal wave. She felt the sting of tears. She gave Kelly a gentle smile. "We should probably get cleaned up."

"I'd love to." Kelly's dark eyes danced.

Something inside Rowan loosened and her body began to heat. "You know there's a no sex rule in this hotel, don't you?"

Kelly's hands began wandering and suddenly Rowan found herself bare from the waist up.

Kelly ran her tongue along Rowan's collar bone. "Who said anything about getting under some hot water?"

Rowan reciprocated by unbuttoning Kelly's jeans. "Lift your hips."

Kelly complied, and Rowan pulled her jeans and underwear down her legs so they pooled around her ankles.

"You mean this?" Rowan moved in on Kelly. She nudged Kelly's knees apart.

"That's exactly what I mean," Kelly said, lacing her fingers into Rowan's long hair. Her mind dissolved at the touch of Rowan's lips.

MUCH LATER, ROWAN was admiring the view of Kelly bare and damp from her shower. Kelly eyed her discarded clothes with a grimace.

"God, I wish I had my luggage," she said, screwing up her face in disgust.

"I've got spares of everything," Rowan said with a smile. She was already fully dressed. She rifled in her duffel for spare underwear and tossed it to Kelly.

Kelly caught it and grinned as she slipped on the underpants. She held up Rowan's bra and laughed outright. "Oh, honey. I'm not going to fill this. I'm just not that stacked."

Rowan snorted a laugh and cupped Kelly's breasts. "You feel just right to me."

"I'm making a mess in your underwear," Kelly said, breathless.

That was like a shot of adrenaline to Rowan's groin. "God. Kell."

Kelly stepped back and Rowan eyed her with a slight frown. "Where are you going?"

"*We* are going out. I need clothes for starters."

Rowan gave a dramatic sigh. "Okay. Fine. Whatever."

Kelly laughed as she slipped on the clothes she'd been wearing. She pulled up the sleeve of Rowan's polo shirt and sniffed it with a happy sigh.

Rowan raised an eyebrow.

"Smells like you," Kelly said sheepishly. "I've always loved your perfume."

"Oh," Rowan said. She leant over and gently nuzzled Kelly's neck. "I love the way you smell. I love the way you look. I love being around you."

Kelly slipped her hand into Rowan's and tugged her toward the door. "More later."

Rowan nodded. "There's no way I'm going to let you out of that promise."

They went back down to reception. There was no sign of the clerk.

Good. I don't think I can look at him without blushing. We broke his rule within ten minutes of checking in. She looked at Kelly. *I'm worried about her. I don't like this world at all. I think there's something* horribly *wrong here.*

They went outside and Rowan slipped on her sunglasses. Kelly quickly followed suit. The greenish tinged sunlight made Kelly look pale and unhealthy.

"Which way do you want to go?" Rowan looked up and down the deserted street.

"Let's keep going past the hotel. I didn't really see anything on the way into town." She glanced at Rowan. "I couldn't stop *looking*, you know?"

"I understand completely," Rowan said. "Why is this place so deserted?" *It feels a lot more desolate than just a quiet country town. And I don't think it should be this quiet anyway. There's something wrong.* She rolled internal eyes. *I'm starting to get sick of hearing myself say that.*

They walked down the street past the pub. A gentle breeze blew, chilling them both to the bone. Dust blew up in eddies on the street.

"Looks like no one's been down this way for a while." Kelly shivered and stepped closer to Rowan.

Rowan put an arm around Kelly's shoulders. "This should all be over by this evening."

"We hope," Kelly muttered.

They walked past another series of vacant shops. This time there were no signs in the windows. It felt as though no one was interested in renting out the commercial spaces. *Well, there's no one here to set up shop, is there?*

After five minutes of walking past vacant lots and desultory houses—these, at least, looked used—they made it to the edge of a parking lot of a store that proudly proclaimed itself to be *Farmer & Co.*

The parking lot was empty except for four cars. They all looked as lackluster as everything else they'd seen so far. The asphalt was ancient and riddled with potholes; the lines marking the spaces were a memory in most places. Yellowish weeds, almost knee high, sprung up through the cracks and around the parking lot flood lights. *I'll best most of those are broken or just, plain, don't work.*

They reached the automatic doors and they slid open with a whoosh. They stepped inside and looked around.

"That way, I think," Kelly said, pointing toward a fading sign that said *Women's Apparel.*

They made their way through half-empty racks of clothing and a dusty jewelry department.

Kelly's eyes lit up when she saw *Ladies Intimates.* She rifled through neat but Spartan racks.

They quickly went through the clothing department and Kelly

found jeans, shirts, and a pair of hiking boots that looked sturdy and in good condition. Rowan found them each a thick coat. They went to the cash register.

The woman behind the counter barely spared them a glance. She rang up their goods on an old cash register. Kelly handed over her card. The woman swiped it, waited a few seconds, and then stared at the screen with a frown.

"No good," she said, handing the card back to Kelly. "Says the card is invalid."

"No problem," Rowan said smoothly before Kelly could say anything. She thrust her card in the woman's direction. Rowan's card worked and in five minutes they left the store.

Kelly was quiet and looked unhappy.

"What's up, Kell?" she asked.

"I don't like the way my card didn't work."

"I don't like it either. But mine did. So we're good. Aren't we?"

Kelly's lips tightened.

"Let it go for now," Rowan said. "You *have* to. If we're really lucky this will all be over soon and we can get on with the rest of our lives tomorrow morning."

"I hope so," Kelly said. "I don't want to live like this."

Rowan felt sad and guilty. "I'm sorry, Kelly."

Kelly pulled her to a halt. "It's okay, Rowan."

"I'm still sorry."

"Don't be," Kelly said. "This is what we got. This is what we deal with."

Rowan nodded and they continued on their way back to the hotel.

I'm so sorry, Kell. I wish we'd left last night.

CHAPTER 12

KELLY'S ROOM WAS much brighter than Rowan's as it was at the end of the hallway toward the front of the hotel. It had bay windows, and the septic sunlight flooded the room.

Kelly stripped off her clothes as Rowan pulled the tags off the new ones. She changed into them, watching Rowan's perfect profile as she stared out of the window into the town around them.

This is a dying world. We can't stay here.

"What do you want to do today?" she asked—her voice as loud as a gunshot in the silent room.

"I was going to ask you the same thing." Rowan turned to her.

Kelly's stomach grumbled and she looked at her watch. The hands stood at just after eleven. "I'm kind of hungry. Let's get a bite to eat."

"Sure," Rowan said. "That sounds good. I'm hungry too."

Kelly sat on the bed beside Rowan and pushed silken strands of Rowan's golden hair out of her face and over her shoulder. "You're beautiful."

Rowan's lips curved into a smile. "So are you."

"I'm scared, Rowan."

Rowan cupped her face with a gentle hand. "No matter what happens, we're together. We'll face everything together."

Kelly tried for a smile. "Thanks, love."

"C'mon." Rowan pulled her to her feet. "Let's go and find some food."

They went downstairs to the pub.

Although it was close to lunch time, there were only about ten people in the hotel. They went into the bistro.

Kelly blinked in the low lighting. The room looked dusty and as lonely as everywhere else, despite the cheerful sports décor.

"Take a seat anywhere, ladies," a woman said from behind the counter. "Do you know what you want?"

"Can I have the special?" Rowan said.

"Make that two," Kelly chimed in.

"Ravioli it is, then," the woman said. "Would you like something to drink?"

"Water for both of us," Rowan said.

"Sorry, love, we don't have any drinking water today. Doesn't come until Monday. You want a Solo?"

"Uh, sure," Kelly said. She held up two fingers.

The woman gave her a brief smile. "I'll be right out with your drinks." She turned away and disappeared behind the counter.

"What the fuck is going on here?" Kelly asked. She felt a deep seated uneasiness that threatened to boil over into full-blown panic.

Rowan quickly took her hand. "Deep breath, love. Deep breath."

Kelly took a deep, shuddering breath and forced herself to relax.

Two glasses banged down on the table between them. Rowan murmured her thanks.

"That's pleasantly odd," she said.

"Which part?" Kelly asked sourly.

"I'm holding your hand and she didn't stare at us."

"That's the *only* thing I like about this world. There's no homophobia. At all."

"I think we should go for a walk around town after we've eaten," Rowan said. "Get the lay of the land."

"I'm not sure I want it."

"It's only going to be for a few hours, love."

"I know." Kelly sighed. She felt remarkably unenthusiastic about the idea of leaving the hotel.

The woman arrived with two small, steaming plates of what looked like canned ravioli.

They waited until she left and dug in. *This* is *canned ravioli. It tastes awful. Kind of metallic. Like the can soaked into the food.*

They were both finished in less than five minutes. Rowan looked as unsettled as she felt.

Rowan leaned forward. "That was horrible. It was like it was spoiled."

"I know," Kelly said. "I don't think it had any meat in it either, which is probably a blessing. Otherwise I think we'd both have food poisoning by now."

Rowan nodded. "Let's pay the bill and get out of here."

Kelly took a long swallow of her Solo and nearly gagged. It tasted almost fishy.

"Yeah, I think it's rotting," Rowan said.

Kelly grimaced.

Rowan picked up the check and her eyes widened.

"What?"

"Thirty dollars."

"What? Let me see."

Rowan handed Kelly the check. They were charged ten dollars each for the food and five each for the drink.

"I'm glad we're out of here today," Kelly said. "This place is a killer."

Rowan nodded.

They got up and Rowan paid the bill.

They went outside into the midday sunshine, and Rowan quickly took Kelly's hand. They went back up the road they'd driven down to get to the hotel. They passed a couple of people who avoided eye contact and paid no attention to their clasped hands.

The shops they passed had barely any merchandise. They passed a news agency and Kelly pulled Rowan to a halt. They looked at the headlines in stands outside, leaning against the walls.

>*DCCC predicts record cold winter.*
>*Record rainfall in Queensland.*
>*Nuclear explosion rocks North America.*

Kelly shivered. Rowan immediately put her arm around her and pulled her in close.

"We'll be gone soon," she said, kissing Kelly's temple. Kelly snuggled into her, glad for her presence.

They kept walking, toward the police station. Now there was a lone police car parked outside. It was dusty and worn. The Australian flag—which didn't have a Union Jack in the corner—hung desultorily from the flagpole.

"I want to get out of here for a few hours," Kelly said. "Let's go and see what Settler's Creek is like. And also the fire pit."

"Okay," Rowan said.

They headed back to the hotel. Rowan tossed Kelly the keys.

Kelly got into the driver's seat and a few moments later they were headed back up the main road out of town and toward the four-way stop sign.

"What do you think happened here?" Kelly asked.

"Something terrible," Rowan said.

Kelly glanced at her. Rowan's eyes were haunted.

"I think it's still going on," Kelly said. "We could live here, Rowan, but we don't belong here."

Rowan nodded. "I know."

The afternoon sunlight was leprous and gave them both an unhealthy appearance. The trees looked as close to death as they had in the morning and the silence was unnerving.

"Have you seen any animals? Birds?" Kelly asked.

Rowan shook her head. "No."

They reached the stop sign and went straight through, down to Settler's Creek. The road started off a wreck with deep potholes, which petered out into a dirt track. The trees drew in closer and closer to the road until there was nothing left but a walking trail.

"You want to go the rest of the way down?" Rowan asked.

Kelly shook her head and eyed the menacing undergrowth. "No. I don't think so."

"I'm kind of glad you said that."

Kelly drove backward until she reached a place she could turn around.

Soon they were headed toward the fire pit.

They saw about twenty soldiers outside the Department of Catastrophe and Climate Change. They seemed worn out and listless, patrolling the edges of the car park with a visible lack of enthusiasm.

They continued on to the fire pit and pulled up into the car park. They got out and looked around.

"This looks exactly the same as it did the last time we were here," Rowan said, frowning.

They walked toward the fire pit, stood at the edge, and looked down into it. The same anemic tree hung over the edge, ancient dust and rotten wood resting in the bottom.

"Check out the monument," Kelly said.

Settler's Creek 1850 - 1902. God rest their souls.

Rowan let out a deep breath. "I guess that settles it, then. We really *have* swapped realities."

"I understand that intellectually," Kelly said, after a moment. Her mind was racing. *How the hell is this happening? How is this even possible? The energy requirements to do that would be more than the universe even has.*

"I have a theory," Rowan said.

"Shoot," Kelly said.

"I think the flashes of light and the *ghosts* we've both been seeing aren't migraines or imagination. I think that's different realities colliding with each other."

Kelly nodded. "Well, that part seems pretty obvious now. You know what the sixty-four thousand dollar question is, don't you?"

"Who's doing it and why?"

Kelly nodded. "Yep." She sighed. "The other big question you should be asking is what happens if we don't get back tonight."

"Why wouldn't we? We successfully crossed realities the past couple of nights."

"That's true but how do you know it's going to happen again tonight? How do you know we didn't just have the rotten luck to land in Settler's Creek on the nights they were running their experiment?"

"Do you think it was Department of Defense that was doing it?"

"I don't know," Kelly said. "Do you remember what Victor said that Glen was saying? A separate lift at the back of the computer room? That there was none? If there was no lift, it means that whoever was doing it wasn't in our reality."

Rowan looked thoughtful for a moment. Fear lurked in her brilliant blue gaze. "That means we got sucked up into someone's experiment."

Kelly nodded. She shrugged. "We have no control over this situation. I *hate* that. I don't like being at the mercy of the government. Big bunch of arseholes."

Rowan nodded.

Kelly walked to the edge of the ridge, to the lookout. A mild breeze blew across the ridge, blowing the fringe off her forehead and chilling her to the bone. She looked down at the plain.

The flat land went on forever. It had a strange, anemic look in the greenish sunlight.

At the base of the ridge, a ghostly town swam into being. It looked transparent. Cars warred with buggies and carts for space on the road.

"It's starting again," Rowan said.

Kelly sighed. "Yeah. Looks like."

"Do you want to go back to the hotel or do you want to stay up here?" Rowan asked.

"Let's go to Settler's Creek Motel," Kelly said. "Every time we've world hopped we've been there. It's probably superstitious but it maximizes our chances of being in the right place when we world hop." She smiled. "But first I want to see the town down there."

Rowan smiled. "All right."

CHAPTER 13

"THIS ISN'T AS easy as I thought it'd be," Kelly said, ducking a branch as they made their way through thick bush toward the ghost town.

Rowan scanned the ground. *No snakes. No insects. How long before this world falls completely apart?*

They broke through a thick stand of dying trees and into a rough clearing.

There were ruins all around them, like they'd seen at Ithaca the previous evening. What was once a main street wound off into the distance ahead of them, dotted by trees and crumbling sandstone and wooden buildings. There was a faint odor of turning fish in the air and Rowan wrinkled her nose.

This place stinks.

There was also an odd overlay of transparent, modern buildings. A ghostly man in jeans and Megadeath tee shirt strolled past them, unseeing. A woman with a pram that could easily have come from eighteen ninety strolled past a man in a top hat, who in turn strolled past a girl texting on a cell phone. Rowan shivered.

Kelly pulled her into motion and they went down the street, dodging specters and in one case, a solid-looking model T Ford.

The sun hung halfway toward the horizon, casting the trees into long shadow.

"We should head back to the motel," Rowan said. Her ever present sense of uneasiness escalated again and she pushed it back.

Kelly gave her a long look. "Okay," she finally said.

They went back up the main street, watching images of people and things fade in and out of reality.

"This doesn't feel like it did the past couple of nights,"

Rowan said. "It's always felt like there was electricity in the air. This feels like nothing."

Kelly was silent a moment. "True."

They climbed back up the bush path toward the car. By the time they'd reached it, it was dusk.

"Do you want to get a bite to eat?" Rowan asked.

Kelly shook her head. "No. No way. I just want to leave."

"All of my luggage is in Ithaca," Rowan said.

"If we snap back to our reality, we're either going to find it in your motel room or it's going to be sitting somewhere in the ruins of Ithaca."

"Is Ithaca in ruins in our world?" Rowan asked as they climbed into the car.

"I don't know, actually," Kelly said. "We never went down there. And I don't know what world we were in when we saw the ruins yesterday."

They drove back up the hill toward Settler's Creek Motel. They passed two trucks of soldiers turning through the stop sign down to Ithaca.

Kelly pulled up into their space in the motel and they went into the remains of Rowan's room. Rowan shook out the sheets and laid them flat on the bed. She got on the bed, pulling Kelly down with her. She slipped her arms around Kelly and pulled her in close.

Kelly gave a bone-cracking yawn. "I'm sorry. We didn't sleep much last night."

"Enjoy it while you can. I plan on repeating our sleep deprivation experiment," Rowan said, yawning.

"Good." Kelly smiled. "I'm hungry, cold and wound up but I'm also so tired I can hardly keep my eyes open."

"I feel like I've been drugged," Rowan said, fighting sleep.

Kelly's eyes had already closed and her breathing was deep and even as she slept.

Rowan wasn't far behind. She closed her eyes and went into oblivion.

ROWAN'S EYES FLUTTERED open. Grey dawn shone into the bay window. She took a deep breath of foul air.

"Oh, shit," she said softly, sitting up. She dislodged Kelly, who was curled up into her.

"What?" Kelly said as her eyes fluttered open. They suddenly widened and she sat up as well. "Oh, no."

Rowan looked around at the ruins of their motel room. "We're still here."

"It didn't happen last night."

They looked at each other, neither one daring to ask the question. *Are we stranded here?*

"What now?" Kelly asked.

"We head back down to Sydney," Rowan said.

Kelly looked at her as though she'd lost her mind. "Don't you want to stay here? See if it happens tonight?"

Rowan slowly shook her head. "That idea's really appealing but it's bad. One thing that occurred to me is that this probably isn't a natural phenomenon. Given the energy requirements to do this at all, it's probably done with intent. That means someone's running an experiment. They've done it for the past couple of nights but not last night. We don't know when they're going to run it again."

"We don't know that they won't do it tonight, either."

"Think about it for a second, Kell," Rowan said gently. "Glen is missing. Someone who *sounded* like him had his cell phone. We found the cell phone and the fatigues here, yesterday morning. That means that our Glen clone is running around in this world somewhere. You remember when we were flying up here? You thought you saw Glen in Brisbane at the airport? Maybe that *was* the Glen from here."

"I'd forgotten about that. You're right. Do you think he's somehow responsible for this?"

"I don't know if it's him personally, but yes, I think he has *something* to do with it."

"We have to find him. Maybe he can tell us what the fuck is going on here."

"Yep," Rowan said. "And I'm guessing, since he has Glen's driver's license, that he headed down to Glen's place. In Sydney."

"How do we even know that there's a Glen in this world at all?"

"We don't." Rowan pulled her up off the bed and they went out to the car. "There's something that's not sitting right about all of this. I'm guessing the owner of the fatigues looked *exactly* like Glen. It was probably an alternate version of him. He's trying to take Glen's place."

"If that's true, then it means he's trying to escape something," Kelly said. She shivered.

"Exactly," Rowan said. "I think Glen's in trouble."

"We have to try and find him."

Rowan nodded. "Yes. We do."

Ten minutes later they pulled up outside the Ithaca Hotel. It looked as desolate and miserable as the day before.

They went upstairs and quickly packed. Kelly went outside to put their luggage in the car while Rowan checked them both out.

The clerk stared at her mistrustfully. "Checking out?"

Rowan nodded. "Yes. Three ten and three twelve."

"Both rooms on the one card?"

Rowan nodded.

He swiped her card. "Where you headed to?"

"Sydney."

"Road to Brisbane is good," the clerk said. "They're forecasting a meteor shower tonight. You might want to hole up before then."

Rowan nodded. She didn't know what he was talking about. He sounded suitably ominous. "Thank you." She accepted the receipt from him.

She jogged out to the car. Kelly was already sitting in the driver's seat and the engine was idling.

"You're not going to like this," Rowan said as she got in. "The clerk said something about a meteor shower tonight. He told us to make sure we were under cover before then."

Kelly shivered. "Shit."

"That's what I thought," Rowan said.

Kelly quickly took them back onto the road that led to the Rockhampton turnoff and God knew what else. They drove past the ruins of the motel and back down toward the ridge. The road was in marginally better repair.

Greenish cirrus clouds hung in the sky, low and threatening. The sky had a hard look to it that was troubling. As they went down the ridge, Kelly slowed the car.

"Look," she said. "The monument to Ithaca is on the other side of the road."

"You want to stop and look?" Rowan asked.

Kelly shook her head. "Not really. I'm suffering from nerves and I just want to get the hell out of here and back to what passes for civilization in this godforsaken world."

"I'm glad you said that," Rowan said. "You take us into Rockie and I'll take us down to Brisbane. Yes?"

Kelly nodded. "Works for me."

An hour later, they were at the turnoff to what she thought of as Settler's Creek. This anemic road sign announced that the turnoff was for *Ithaca*. There was a smaller sign for *The Department of Catastrophe and Climate Change* under that.

There was a petrol station and Kelly pulled into it. Rowan got out and stretched. She felt Kelly looking at her. She was blushing.

"I'm sorry, Rowan," she said. "My card doesn't work on the bowsers."

"Oh." Rowan dug her wallet out of her pocket. "I'm sorry. I didn't think."

She swiped her card and Kelly began to fuel up.

"I'm going to go inside and see if I can get us something to snack on," Rowan said.

Kelly gave her a thumbs up.

Rowan went into the small convenience store. Most of the shelves were empty. There were a few dusty car parts hanging on the walls. The clerk ignored her, focusing on the television before her. It was blaring out the weather channel.

Rowan went to the refrigerators at the back of the store. Most of those shelves were empty as well. There were three bottles of water left on the bottom shelf. Rowan grabbed them and went to the counter.

The shelves before the counter were also bare.

Rowan cleared her throat.

The clerk looked up at her, staring suspiciously.

"I'll have these. Do you have any food?"

"What do we look like, a supermarket?" the clerk said, scanning the items. "Ten dollars."

Rowan felt her temper flare. "Here." She tossed a bill at the clerk.

"Very funny," the clerk said, turning the bill over. "Now how about you pay for your goods?"

No Union Jack on the flag. Wonder if that means this isn't or wasn't a British colony? Makes sense that they wouldn't take money with the Queen on it, then.

"Here," she said, tossing her credit card at the clerk.

The clerk swiped the card and handed it and the receipt back to her without looking up.

"Thank you," Rowan said.

The clerk ignored her. She was already engrossed in the weather channel again.

She headed out to the car and almost bumped into Kelly heading into the convenience store.

"What gives?" Rowan asked.

"Pump cut out after thirty dollars."

Rowan glanced back at the convenience store. "How much did you get out of it?"

"Pretty close to full."

"Good enough to reach Rockhampton," Rowan said. "I wouldn't bother going in there. She's a bitch. There's no food. I got the last of the water."

"Fuck," Kelly muttered as they headed back to the car. "This is a shitty world, isn't it? There's no living here."

Rowan shook her head as they pulled back out onto the deserted highway. "No. Not at all."

She stared out of the window as Kelly took them down the

highway. They didn't pass any other cars. They shot past a few overgrown farms.

"Pull up into the next farm," Rowan said.

"Why?" Kelly asked, putting out her turn signal as they hit the edges of a town. All the houses looked deserted.

"You'll see," Rowan said as the pulled up into a driveway of a brick house.

It was well built and would have been beautiful if every single window hadn't been broken. The front and back doors stood wide open and a hoist with broken wire leant at a drunken angle past the edge of the house.

Rowan got out of the car and went into the house, Kelly silently following her. The floor was marble covered in a thick layer of dust. The rooms they could see were completely bare.

"You want to check upstairs?" Rowan said. "We're looking for newspapers, books, anything."

Kelly nodded and cautiously made her way up the stairs.

Rowan checked each of the downstairs rooms. The formal dining room was dusty and empty. The walls were water stained and smelt moldy with a now familiar dull undertone of turning fish.

The living room was next, bare of furniture. The den had collapsed shelves and a rotting television set.

The last room left was the kitchen and Rowan steeled herself for more nothing. She blinked in surprise. The sink was full of dirt and the counters were covered in shredded paper. A long disused refrigerator sat in its alcove, unplugged, with the cord holding the door open slightly. She pulled the door the rest of the way open, and was surprised to find that it was simply empty.

The door caught her attention. Her hand was on a faded newspaper clipping.

The end of the world? Screamed the headline.

"Rowan?" Kelly called. "Where are you?"

"In the back. In the kitchen."

Rowan scanned the article. Most of the newsprint was faded into illegibility, but it seemed to be talking about some kind of plague. There was also a single word that stood out. *Meteor.*

"I didn't find anything," Kelly said.

Rowan jumped.

"I'm sorry, I didn't mean to startle you," Kelly said.

"It's all right, love. I'm just as jumpy as you are." Rowan pointed to the clipping. "Check that out."

Kelly gazed at the newsprint. "Shit," she said softly. "Plague? Meteors?" She looked at Rowan, her dark eyes wide. "We really should get the fuck out of here, shouldn't we?"

Rowan nodded. "Yes. Hell yes."

They jogged back out to the car and Kelly backed out onto the road.

They drove through the town at the legal limit. It looked completely deserted. *Everything* looked long abandoned and was falling apart.

"That horrible feeling I had is getting worse," Kelly said.

"And there we were strolling around outside yesterday. Oh, my god," Rowan said.

Kelly drove as fast as she dared toward Rockhampton. They barely passed any other cars on the trip. Almost all of the farms and towns they passed were abandoned wrecks.

They finally pulled up into the outskirts of Rockhampton, and both were more than a little relieved to see more signs of life.

Compared to the loneliness of the past four hours, this was a veritable treasure trove of activity and life. They passed at least five people on their way to the airport. Kelly turned onto Hunter Street and they went into the airport.

"Just pull up into the normal parking lot," Rowan said.

"Yeah, I noticed," Kelly said. "We haven't heard any air traffic, have we?"

Rowan shook her head. "I don't hold out a lot of hope for us getting a flight to Brisbane. I think we're going to end up driving."

Kelly nodded. "Agreed."

They parked and Rowan dug into the glove box to find her rental agreement. "Good," she said as she scanned it. "I got the car until Monday. So we can drop it off tomorrow."

"Nice," Kelly said, slipping her hand into Rowan's as they headed into the terminal.

The terminal seemed a hive of activity, after all the desolation they'd seen. There were three security guards wandering around aimlessly and the entrance to the departure gates was roped off. The departure lounges were dark. There were no signs of any planes on the tarmac.

Rowan spotted the information desk close to the Ansett counters.

"Ansett didn't collapse here," Kelly said.

Rowan nodded.

"Excuse me," Rowan said to the woman sitting behind the desk.

The woman stared off into space.

"Excuse me," Rowan said, a little louder.

The woman started. "Oh, sorry. I wasn't paying attention." She smiled. "What can I do for you?"

"Do you know if there are any flights to Brisbane?"

"No. We've battened down the hatches for the meteor storm tonight. Where are you headed?"

"Brisbane."

The woman winced. "Cutting it close, aren't you? You should wait it out here."

Rowan shook her head. "I can't."

"All right, then. If I were you I'd call ahead to the Old Treasury Hotel in Brisbane. See if they have something for the night. And if they do, get down there as fast as you can."

"I plan to," Rowan said. "Can you give me the number?"

"Sure." The woman swiveled toward her computer screen and moved the mouse and typed rapidly. She grabbed a small piece of paper and wrote down the number.

Rowan accepted the slip of paper. "Thanks."

Kelly was watching all the people in the terminal. She looked tense. "Whatever you're going to do, do it fast. I don't like this at all."

"Neither do I," Rowan said, pulling them over to the public telephones, into a quiet corner.

She called the hotel. They had a room available and Rowan quickly booked it.

"We're out of here. I got us a room and we have to be there

by five. Looks like they're going to close their doors for the night by six." She looked at her watch. It was ten thirty. "Let's fill up and go."

Kelly was already pulling her into motion. They jogged out of the terminal and back to the car. It had gotten noticeably darker outside and the sky had taken on a greenish tinge that was distinctly sickening to look at.

They quickly filled up at a crowded petrol station at the edge of town, and began the long trip to Brisbane.

CHAPTER 14

PURPLISH GREEN CLOUDS covered the sky from horizon to horizon by the time they'd reached Brisbane.

Kelly looked at her watch. It'd stopped. She looked at the dashboard clock. It was flashing twelve.

She frowned and looked at Rowan's watch. Hers was still running. It was coming up to four thirty.

"We're headed to the Treasury Casino, aren't we?" she asked.

"Yep. I recognize the address."

Kelly caressed Rowan's thigh. "How are you doing?"

"I'm okay. Bit stiff but I'm fine." Rowan smiled. "Looking forward to you and a big bed tonight."

Kelly laughed. "Terminally horny?"

"Always have been around you, Kell. I think you're incredibly hot."

They drove down into the Brisbane central business district and followed the signs to The Old Treasury Hotel. Purple lightning flashed in the sky.

"I didn't know that. If I'd known I'd have started something with you much earlier," Kelly said.

"I never thought you'd ever notice me. I never thought you'd ever want me."

Kelly snorted a laugh. "You honestly never noticed I couldn't stop staring at your breasts?"

"Probably because I was too busy staring at your butt and wondering what you looked like under your clothes."

They made the turn into the underground car park.

The car park was only half full. Kelly hadn't been expecting any more. There were more people in Brisbane. It was a city but the small population made it seem more like a large town.

Rowan pulled up into a spot and got out of the car. She stretched and her spine cracked. Kelly winced.

"I'm fine," Rowan said. "Just not a car designed for someone of my height."

"Then why did you rent it?"

"I don't know. I'll remember to ask myself when I see me."

Kelly laughed.

They went up to reception. There were more people in the foyer but it didn't feel crowded.

Kelly went to the glass front doors and looked out.

The sky was a threatening grayish green, lit up by purple flashes of light. Smoke trails followed some of the flashes.

"You'll be safe here, miss," a male voice said from right beside her.

She jumped. "Excuse me?"

"I said, you'll be safe here, miss," the middle-aged bellboy said, standing beside her. "This isn't supposed to be a big one, anyway. Only last an hour or so. Not predicted to do any damage." He gestured toward the upper floors. "We reinforced the building a few years ago after the big one that killed all those people."

"Oh." Kelly wanted to ask what *the big one* was but didn't know how. His demeanor suggested that the event was common knowledge.

"Ready, love?" Rowan asked, standing beside her.

"As I'll ever be." She accepted Rowan's kiss.

The bellboy bent and took Rowan's duffel. He led them to the elevator. "Where to, miss?"

"Second floor. Room two forty."

"Off we go, then."

A few minutes later they were in their room. Kelly looked at the window. It was triple reinforced glass and the frame looked like tempered steel. She shivered. The room itself was beautiful, considering the world they were in. The carpet was thick and only slightly worn in places; the sheets were clean and the bed looked soft and inviting.

The television was on and playing a warning.

The meteor storm is starting. Go indoors immediately for your own safety. Stay away from windows and doors unless you are in a reinforced building. Repeat. The meteor storm is starting. Seek shelter at once. Shut off all nonessential electrical equipment. A further broadcast will be made when it is safe to go outdoors.

"Room service will be up in ten minutes," Rowan said. She slipped her arms around Kelly's waist and began nibbling her neck.

Kelly tilted her head back so it was resting on Rowan's shoulder. Rowan kept up her nipping kisses as her hands wandered along the planes and curves of Kelly's body.

By the time room service arrived, Kelly was half naked and her body throbbed unmercifully. She broke Rowan's kiss and backed away slightly, wanting nothing more than to tear off her clothes. Rowan's eyes were hot and she seemed to be dragging her gaze from Kelly's breasts to her face.

"I have to get that. Neither one of us ate anything and I don't know about you, but I'm starved."

Kelly pulled on her tee shirt.

Rowan opened the door and a man pushing a cart came in just as an explosion sounded in the distance. He paid no attention.

Kelly watched a ball of fire sail down out of the clouds and explode on the ground some distance away.

"Please stay away from the windows, miss," he said as Rowan signed the slip. "For your safety."

Kelly nodded. "Got it."

They waited for him to leave and Rowan pulled off the lid covering one of the plates.

It was just a plate of canned spaghetti and what looked like green meatballs, but Kelly's hunger roared to life.

"I don't care if it *is* canned. I'm so hungry."

Rowan grinned and handed her the plate. "It was the best they had, love."

They ate their canned food. There was a lot of it and Kelly felt pleasantly full when they were finished. Rowan handed her a small cup of lemon sorbet and Kelly ate that with gusto.

"I asked for chocolate but they didn't have any," Rowan said. "Otherwise I would have put it all over your body and licked it off."

Kelly's libido sprang back to life. She put down her empty cup and advanced on Rowan.

Soon they were tangled together on the bed and Rowan was crying out her orgasm, clutching convulsively at the sheets.

The explosions continued with increasing frequency and the room was lit up with orange light.

Rowan flipped her over onto her back and began to kiss and nip her all over. Kelly was soon snuggled in Rowan's arms, trying to catch her breath, body twitching from her orgasm.

There was a thunderous explosion and the room lit up bright as day with firelight.

"What the fuck," Kelly said, quickly getting out of bed and looking out of the window.

"What is it?" Rowan asked from the bed.

Kelly looked at the ground below. "Something hit the building across the road from us. Whatever it was is glowing purple and green."

"What?"

Meteors rained down from the sky, crashing into the ground below. There was an explosion high above them and the building creaked.

The television crackled to life. *There is no cause for alarm. The building is safe at this time. There is no cause for alarm. The building is safe at this time.*

The announcement droned on and on, repeating the same thing over again. Kelly glanced around and saw Rowan turning down the volume.

She turned back to the window. "Look at this."

She felt the heat from Rowan's body behind her, felt the entire length of her long, sensual body pressed up against hers. She felt

Rowan's large breasts pressing into her back and swallowed. Rowan's arms slipped around her waist and she realized with dim amazement that she actually felt *safe*.

"Look at that," Rowan said. "Are those men in metal suits going over to the meteor?"

"And spraying foam on it."

The meteor immediately dimmed but it looked as though the damage had already been done. The ground was glowing. It was an ugly shade of yellow that sank into the debris beneath the meteor.

"Is the ground being poisoned by those things?" Rowan said.

"I'm guessing yes. That'd explain why there's no food."

"Or very little. Wonder how long this has been going on for?"

"There aren't many people around. This is a city. I'd expect more people. I'm guessing a whole bunch of people died in the big meteor storm."

"And those left are probably dying of starvation."

"This has been going on for years," Kelly's mind whirled. "You saw the houses we passed today. You saw the newspaper article on the fridge in that empty house. It was years since anyone lived there." She turned to Rowan. "You know what I think?"

Rowan studied her. "What?"

"I think that people are finally recovering from these meteor storms. Civilization is teetering on the brink of collapsing, but it hasn't yet. I'm guessing that someone's coming up with a way to grow plants underground or underwater or something. You noticed there's no meat? Well, pasta is made from flour and water. I've *never* seen green meatballs and I don't think this world has had them all along. I'm guessing that food production is slowly coming back." She shivered. "But I also still think this world is dying."

Rowan's gaze turned inward for a moment. Her eyes widened. "I haven't seen any kids, have you?"

Kelly almost unwillingly shook her head. "I think we're on a dying world. They survived a cataclysm but now everyone's sterile."

Rowan pulled her back to the bed and they lay down together.

"We're not in other *worlds*, we're in other *realities*," Rowan said. "What happened at that fire pit in Settler's Creek? That, I think, is the focal point of these realities."

"What do you mean?"

"You know that old idea that a butterfly beating its wings in China produces a tidal wave in Africa?"

"I've heard that. I can't remember what the chain of logic there actually is but I know it's a cascading sequence of action and reaction that creates the final outcome. When we got to site, it was Settler's Creek that survived the bushfire. The reality we're in now is the one where *Ithaca* survived the fire. Wonder which one survived in the world where the god squad was in charge?"

Rowan snorted a laugh. "I don't know." She turned serious again. "First, I think we've found our proof of multiple realities. Second, neither one of us belongs here. We *have* to find Glen and find some way to get home."

"I feel trapped." Kelly snuggled into Rowan's broad shoulder. "I don't want to play this game anymore. I want to go home."

"You and me both." Rowan twisted so she was looking into Kelly's eyes. "We are in this together. As long as we keep talking to each other, we'll be fine. It's the same as it's been for the past few days. You and me against the world."

"I'm worried, Rowan." Kelly forced the words out of the deepest recesses of her soul. "I think I don't exist in this world. I'm completely dependent on you. What happens if something happens to you? What happens if you decide you don't want to be with me anymore? I'm well and truly stuck. I can't rent a car and drive back up to Settler's Creek. I can't go home. If I get sick I can't go to a doctor. I'm well and truly *screwed.*"

Rowan tightened her arms around her and Kelly felt the sting of tears.

"This isn't a game for me, Kell. I love you. I want to be with you. You can have me for as long as you want me. I'm *not* going anywhere. As for being dependent on me, maybe so. I can see you staying with me and I can see myself coming home to you. But you're *not* my slave. I expect nothing of you."

"I've *never* been good with being dependent on anyone."

"What's mine is yours, Kell. We're equals."

"I don't *want* to be domestic. I like being a working woman."

"Hey, hey, hey," Rowan said softly, cupping Kelly's chin and forcing her to meet her eyes. "Relax. I'm not expecting you to turn into a housewife. I fully expect you to do whatever the hell you want until we find Glen and get the hell out of here. Don't be afraid of me, Kelly. There's no reason to be."

Kelly began to cry. "It's not that I don't trust you, Rowan. That's not it. It's just that when I see us together, you're in your office and I'm in mine. I *want* to work. I *want* to contribute. I just don't know how this is going to work."

Rowan held her close. "*Neither* of us belongs here. We just have to work out some way to get home."

"I'm sorry, Rowan. I'm so sorry."

"Don't be, love. Don't be. Believe it or not, I *do* get what you're saying to me."

"I know you do." *How long are we going to be stuck here for?*

Rowan held her and let her cry herself out. She kissed away Kelly's tears and they made love again. Rowan was gentle with her and Kelly felt her love in the way they touched and kissed.

Kelly fell into a deep sleep in the comforting circle of Rowan's arms.

CHAPTER 15

THE NEXT MORNING they were on the road back down to Sydney again. Kelly was behind the wheel and Rowan was leaning back in the passenger seat, staring out of the window at the sick undergrowth.

"I'm sorry about last night," Kelly said.

Rowan looked at her, surprised. "Why? Why should you apologize for telling me what you need?"

"I know none of that's what you wanted to hear."

"You *have* to tell me these things, love. You *have* to."

They pulled into the petrol station in Ballina. The parking lot of the Big Prawn was deserted. Rowan got out and began to fuel up.

Kelly felt her face heat. "You got a couple of bucks? Maybe I can get us some coffee."

Rowan smiled and handed her a debit card and gave her the PIN number. "I meant to tell you. Yesterday I tried paying for the water on the Capricorn Highway with cash. Didn't work. May as well be monopoly money. In this reality Australia doesn't have the queen on her bills."

Kelly frowned. "Serious?"

Rowan laughed. "Um, *yes.*"

Kelly shook her head and went into the café next to the petrol station convenience store. A woman stood behind the counter, waiting for business.

"Help you?" she asked as Kelly approached.

"Coffee?" Kelly asked.

The woman glared at her. "What does this look like? A five star restaurant? You get Koff, just like everyone else."

"Thanks," Kelly said. "Two, please."

The woman made her beverage and Kelly used Rowan's debit card, feeling guilty as she did it.

She brought them back to the car just as Rowan was screwing on the fuel cap.

"This is something called Koff." Kelly handed her the drink. "I don't know how it tastes. I don't know anything about it at all, including how to prepare it so it tastes good."

Rowan gamely took a sip and screwed up her face. "Wow. Bitter. Woody. Nutty. Not to my taste at all."

Kelly took a cautious sip and almost spat it out. "Holy shit. That's not to my taste either."

"Maybe milk would help it but I haven't seen any cows around."

"Yeah."

They continued down the road.

IT WAS LATE in the afternoon when they finally hit the exit from the Newcastle Freeway—called the Sydney Expressway in this reality—and drifted onto the Pacific Highway.

Traffic was as Spartan there as it was everywhere else. The houses looked broken down or deserted. Some seemed to be empty. There were empty convenience stores and dilapidated train stations. The one train they saw looked like it'd been in service since the first quarter of the century. Rowan kept her eyes steadfastly on the road, avoiding potholes, and in half an hour they reached the Sydney Harbor Bridge.

Rowan began to dig into her pockets for change, but Kelly quickly stopped her.

"What?" she asked. "I need change for the toll."

"There's no toll booths."

"Nice." Rowan drove by the remains of the concrete blocks that had once held toll booths. "Geez, look at the water." It was a troubling shade of purple and crystal clear. It looked almost empty except for mammoth fish things moving under the surface.

"What are those?" Kelly asked just as a dorsal fin slipped above the water.

"I think they were maybe sharks once upon a time," Rowan said, careful to keep her eyes trained on the road. The water made her feel sick. The Harbour Bridge was faded and rusty and she hoped it would stay upright for the few seconds it took them to cross it.

One of the shells that made up the Opera House had collapsed and the Opera House itself looked derelict. It was roped off. The Royal Botanic Gardens were choked by mutant weeds and yellow grass.

They took the Cahill Expressway toward the Eastern Suburbs. They passed skyscrapers that looked old and damaged. The remains of weather-stained plastic hung from some windows. Some of the other buildings had holes; they looked as though they'd been bombed.

"I wonder if Town Hall is as nasty as this?" Kelly asked.

"I don't know," Rowan said. "I looked at one of my business cards and it looks like I work in Surry Hills. The building before we moved to the one close to Circular Quay."

"That old dump? The one with no parking?"

"I don't think parking is going to be a problem and every building here seems to be a dump."

"I wish I could disagree with you."

Rowan cut across Macquarie Street, heading to George Street so they could see the city close up.

There were more people around, she noted with relief. Most of them looked thin and listless but it was somehow comforting to see more faces. Kelly gently squeezed her thigh and Rowan kissed her knuckles.

There wasn't much traffic and the trip down George Street was fast. Most of the buildings in the city looked as rundown as the farm houses they'd passed from Settler's Creek to Sydney. They drove past a cathedral that looked as though it'd been in ruins even before anything else that had happened to change the world.

"Look at that. Looks like it hasn't been used since Federation," Kelly said.

Rowan nodded. "I know. That's odd. That's not the only church I've seen that looks like the flock scattered."

"I know. The mosque outside Coffs looked like that as well."

"Hah," Rowan said. "That's odd." *Does anyone believe in*

God anymore here? Well, Australia's biggest religion was always atheism, I guess.

They made it back to Rowan's house in Maroubra in half an hour. She pulled up into the driveway behind her familiar company car with a broad sense of relief.

"Do you want me to take you home or do you want to stay with me?" Rowan asked, peering at Kelly.

"I don't want to go to my place. I don't want to find out I don't live there. I want to stay with you. I *need* to be with you."

"Come with me," Rowan said.

She pulled her duffel out of the back of the car and dug in her pocket for her house keys. Kelly was straight behind her and it felt strange. *Good* strange. If she was honest with herself, she'd wanted to be Kelly's lover from almost the first time they'd met. She'd *wanted* to come home to Kelly. She had always felt perfectly comfortable imagining Kelly leaning against her kitchen counter, sipping coffee; Kelly waking up in her bed; Kelly snuggled against her as they ate breakfast on a Saturday morning.

I just never wanted it to happen this way. If she ever talks to me again after this is all over I'll be surprised.

"Are you going to open the door?" Kelly asked.

Rowan felt her face heat. "Huh? Yeah."

Kelly looked at her curiously. "Why are you blushing?"

Because I want to carry you over the threshold. "Uh. I don't know how clean it is in here."

"Ah." Kelly smiled. "Don't worry about me. That's the bottom of our list of things to worry about."

"Okay." Rowan pushed the door open and gestured for Kelly to go ahead of her.

"Wow," Kelly said. "This is beautiful."

Rowan looked around the foyer of her house. It felt eerily familiar and completely foreign.

There were reproductions of Monet all over the walls and a small hall table by the left wall. The living room was to the right. *Look at that. In this reality I took the blue leather sofa and recliners. That looks better than the cloth ones do. That's one hell of a big living room. And look at all those painted female nudes. I must be a real hound dog in this reality.*

"Got enough pictures of naked women lying around?" Kelly sounded distinctly unimpressed.

Uh, oh. "It's me in this reality, Kell. It's not the *me* you know and love."

"I'll try and remember that."

Rowan dropped her duffel in the living room and they went into the kitchen. *Yellow walls and pictures of daisies. This time Van Gogh. I have to admit it looks a hell of a lot more cheerful in here.*

Rowan cautiously opened the refrigerator. She suppressed a sigh of relief. It was fanatically neat and clean and packed with water.

"Your cupboards are stuffed with canned food," Kelly said.

Rowan looked at Kelly. She was systematically opening all the cupboard doors. The crockery was eerily familiar, the same dishes painted with green fish as she had in her own kitchen.

They went into the hallway from the left door to the kitchen. There was a small, modern bathroom with bright red-and-blue striped towels hanging on the towel racks. Rowan noted with relief that there was only one toothbrush in the holder.

They went back up the hallway to the master bedroom.

This is awesome. I knocked down the wall between here and the first guest bedroom. And I got myself that king size water bed. And another *nude hanging over it. For God's sake, doesn't this me think about anything other than getting laid?*

Kelly experimentally pushed on the bed and gentle waves rippled across the surface. "Nice."

Rowan forgot about everything. She advanced on Kelly and kissed her hard. She pushed Kelly down onto the bed and they knew nothing but each other.

GREEN SUNLIGHT FLOODED the kitchen and Kelly debated whether or not to close the kitchen blinds.

She heard Rowan pad into the kitchen and turned to look

at her. Her heart skipped a beat. Rowan wore a brief robe that barely concealed anything, and Kelly could see flashes of her smooth skin. She toweled her long hair dry.

"You're so beautiful," Kelly whispered, stealing a kiss. "I love you."

Rowan smiled, her bright, blue eyes twinkling with pleasure. "I love you, too." She gestured toward herself apologetically. "I have to get dressed. I have to drop off the car at the airport before work and that means I have to get moving."

"No problem," Kelly said. "Wait. How do you plan on getting to work and home?"

"I'll catch a cab to work. I'll give you a call when I'm ready this afternoon. You can use the company car. Or my car. I'm easy. Keys to both are here." She opened one of the cupboards and pointed to a small rack with neatly labeled keys. "I'm aiming to get to work at eight and leave at five. Should be plenty of time to find Glen."

Kelly nodded. "Fair enough, but you do realize I can't legally drive? I don't have a driver's license here."

Rowan winced. "Okay. Don't break any road rules and you'll be fine."

"And I don't have a phone."

"No problem. I've got a work cell and I seem to have my personal cell here as well. Take that." She put her arms around Kelly and gave her a gentle squeeze. "I'm sorry. I know you hate this."

Kelly squeezed her back. "Thanks, Rowan."

Rowan gave her a gentle kiss on the cheek. "What do you plan on doing today?"

She released Kelly and went into the bedroom to dress. Kelly followed her.

Kelly folded her arms and leant in the doorway, admiring Rowan's muscular form. "I'm going to try and find out what happened to me and I'm going to try to smoke out Glen. If he's even here."

"I'm going to find out the last time he was at work. I might be able to tap into his personnel records and find his address."

"That'll work." Kelly watched as Rowan tucked a sheer blouse into a pair of expensive jeans. "You said something about my seeing Glen in Brisbane. You do realize that it wasn't in this reality, don't you?"

Rowan gaped at her. "Shit. No. I'm an idiot."

Kelly smiled. "I could have been mistaken. The fatigues we found in this world indicate he's probably here somewhere."

Rowan, now fully dressed, stood in front of her. "I'd rather stay here today with you." She looked sad.

"I'd rather you stayed here as well, but this world runs the same as any other. We need money to survive."

Rowan sighed. "I know." She led the way back into the kitchen and went to a jar on the counter. She opened the lid and her eyes lit up in pleasure. She grinned at Kelly. "Well, at least I'm predictable. I still have a jar of money."

"Nice." Kelly smiled. "You'd better go." She nodded toward the clock.

"Hey," Rowan said, slipping her arms around Kelly's waist and kissing her. "It's going to be all right. We *are* going to get out of here, I promise." She smiled and brushed a strand off Kelly's forehead. "Help yourself to anything in my wardrobe. What's mine is yours. Nothing in this house is off limits. I have nothing to hide."

"Thanks, love." She kissed Rowan.

Rowan caressed her face, grabbed her briefcase and car keys and left.

A few seconds later she heard the soft sound of an engine. She looked out of the front windows and watched Rowan as she drove up the street.

She's only been gone about ten seconds and I already miss her.

She went into the bedroom and began opening the drawers. *Okay, we have underwear. We have tee shirts—expensive ones. Ah, jackpot—a drawer full of fresh jeans.* There was a hamper by the dresser almost filled to the top with clothes. *And I should probably do laundry.*

She went into the bathroom and spotted two toothbrushes.

One of them was brand new. Kelly almost guiltily felt herself unclench. She didn't want to know about any other lovers. She couldn't stand the thought of any other woman touching Rowan.

She pulled the shower curtain back and frowned at the tap handles. *Those look weird.* She backed out of the bathroom and let herself out of the back door. The backyard was as neat as the front and perfectly groomed. The grass was an ugly shade of yellow and had a terrible *vibrancy* to it that made her feel uneasy. The plants—roses, a lemon tree in the back corner, and some Grevillias scattered in between—were at once completely familiar and completely foreign. They looked *almost* normal; leaves were of the right shape but a little longer than they should have been; the rose petals were harshly elegant; the scent coming off the roses was strong and had a stomach-turning undertone of something namelessly unpleasant.

She hurried up the side path and around the side of the house to the outside of the bathroom. She frowned. A small, ugly, industrial tank sat in the garden bed below the window. It looked harsh, sturdy, and unappealing. Water pipes led up into it, and black plastic went into the shower, toilet and bathroom sink. She bent over the tank and hesitantly put a hand on it. It was gently vibrating and she saw the ghost of a light flashing against the brickwork of the house. She leant around the other side, trying to see the source of the light. There were three lights and a small LCD display covered in thick plastic. The lights were labeled *Expired, Needs Changing* and *OK.* The *OK* light was flashing green and the small LCD display was blank.

You can't drink the water here. I didn't realize that it needed a heavy duty purification system. I wonder what happens if you drink unpurified water?

She stood slowly. She felt as though she was being watched. She looked around but couldn't see anyone.

She awkwardly made her way around the house to the back door and let herself in again.

A small voice at the back of her mind told her to look out again.

"Jesus Christ." She jumped back, heart hammering.

Every single one of the plants looked like it was leaning toward the back door.

"Oh, Christ. What the hell is going on here?"

CHAPTER 16

AFTER KELLY HAD showered and eaten something from a can called *Breakfast Bread*, she explored the house. She went into the second bedroom. It was clearly an office, with a bed made with dusty sheets tucked into the corner as an afterthought.

There was a large executive desk with a laptop on it, and she powered it up and guiltily opened drawers. There were a cluster of pens, pencils, and other stationary scattered through the drawers, along with half used notepads and a shelf of software CDs. Kelly opened the filing drawers and they were filled with Rowan's paperwork.

I shouldn't do this. It's a gross invasion of her privacy.

She rifled through one called *bank* and pulled out the top one from *St George Building Society.*

Her eyes widened as she scanned it and saw the balance. *Holy mother of god, she's a millionaire.* She put the statement back and found another folder called *financial statements.* She read through them. *She's making a mint off Octahedron. Looks like she owns almost twenty percent of Octahedron.*

She shoved the paper back into the folder and began closing the drawer. She saw a flash of black vinyl behind the file folders.

She glanced at the laptop and logged in. *Thank God there's no password on this or I'd be in trouble.* She reached behind the file folders and pulled out an old address book. *Oh, shit. I'm not sure I want to do this.* She put it flat on the desk and stared at it. *I'm going to find out more than I want to know. I know it's not my Rowan.* She opened it with shaking hands.

The whole address book was littered with cell numbers from other women. Most of the numbers were faded. *Maybe she doesn't use this anymore. Maybe it's just a reminder of her younger days.* The spine of the address book was worn and creased, and it looked as though Rowan had thumbed through the book many times. She felt a wave of jealousy flood over her and her face heated. *How many of these women does she still contact? How many does she touch? If this is what* this *Rowan is like, what's* mine *really like? How long are we going to last for? I'm so fucked.*

She put away the address book and quietly shut the door, waves of pain and humiliation washing over her. *She says she loves me. But for how long? I'm useless here. I can't bring anything to the table.*

The other filing drawer had framed pictures in it.

She pulled out a few. One was of a smiling Rowan in a graduation cap and gown, waving a diploma. Others were of her with a group of people that looked like her—her family.

The last were three framed photographs of Rowan and another woman. She was as beautiful as Rowan and had bright red hair. They were smiling at the mystery photographer. Rowan looked so *happy.* One of the pictures had the ghost of a lipstick kiss on the picture under the glass. Another had an inscription.

You're The One. Love you always, Karen.

Kelly felt as though she'd been torn in half. *Is Karen in our world? Is she headed into Rowan's life in our reality?*

Her vision blurred and she wiped impatiently at her face. She was crying. She carefully put the pictures back and closed the drawer with a sigh.

She leant back in the chair and closed her eyes.

I have to get home. I don't know if Rowan's going to want to come with me. She has a life here if she wants one. She's got lots of money and she's beating other women off with sticks. She owns her own house. What could I possibly offer her?

She forced her melancholy thoughts to one side. It was more urgent to find Glen. She thought about the plants outside and felt a quick stab of fear and relief that she was inside the house and they were outside.

She studied the links on the laptop desktop.

Christ, she's got an address book here as well. And it's over a meg in size. I don't want to know. Now or ever. I'm going to ask her about it. I'm not being fair to her if I don't.

She opened a web browser and the Google home page displayed. She went to the white pages.

Her search for Glen Adams brought back no results. *He could be unlisted. It was worth a shot.*

She hesitated a moment. *I don't think I'm going to be able to do this, but what the hell, we'll give it a whirl.*

Her next search was for birth certificates.

A list of results came back a second or so later.

Holy shit. They post this stuff online. Is there no privacy here? That's on the list to find out why.

She checked the links. *Interesting. Some of these are to the Ministry of Births and Deaths, some are for something called The Registry.*

She began opening pages and reading.

ROWAN WALKED OUT of terminal and looked at the parking structure across the road. It was badly damaged. Someone had taken the time to clear away the rubble. Yellow caution tape flapped listlessly in the stinking breeze. *That happened a while ago. It's still roped off. I doubt anyone is going to rebuild that.*

She went out to the taxi stand. Taxis were lined up and the queue was short.

She leant into the window of the front cab. "You mind taking me to Surry Hills?"

The cab driver was Chinese. He looked thin and sickly. He gave her a sharp nod.

"Thanks." She smiled and got into the cab. He turned on the meter and pulled away from the curb.

Rowan watched the city go past. She tried not to see what it was really like. *Kelly's right. I want to go home.* She sighed at the thought of Kelly, the worry she felt coming to the fore again. *I love her. I hate what's happening to her. It's going to kill her by slow inches staying here. Everything I love so much about her will wither and die if we stay.*

The cab turned onto Elizabeth Street. The traffic became slightly heavier, but still more like on a weekend morning than rush hour on a Monday.

How can I help her?

She thought about what Kelly had said to her. Kelly was right. If anything happened to her, Kelly's life was over. A fierce wave of emotion broke over her. *No matter what, I promise you I'll find some way to get us home.*

The cab pulled up in front of a dilapidated building. *Yuck. I'd forgotten how much I hated working in Surry Hills.*

She paid the cab driver and went to the dirty glass doors with a sigh. She got out her swipe card and noticed the lock was broken. *Figures.*

She let herself in and jogged up the stairs toward where she hoped her office was. She was struck at how worn and decrepit the office space was. The floor was covered in linoleum, worn down the floor boards in places. Almost every step creaked. The open space that held the technicians cubicles had worn carpet tiles on the floors. Most of the cubes were completely bare and covered in a layer of dust; there were few chairs and those that were there had torn fabric and deeply worn seats.

Rowan saw her office and suppressed a sigh of relief. *Thank God that's where it always used to be.*

She took the long way around, walking past what had once been Glen's cubicle. She paused briefly to look at it.

There was a notepad square in the center of the desk with a pen tossed haphazardly on top of it. The laptop docking station was empty and the monitor was off. There was less dust on the keyboard and mouse than in the other cubicles. *He's been here recently. Probably before the site visit.*

"Can I help you, boss?"

"Huh?" Rowan looked up and tried not to look shocked.

A tall and cadaverous Rich Brennan leant on the edge of the cube. He wore jeans, joggers, and a polo shirt. His face was deeply lined and there was a wariness in his eyes she hadn't seen before.

"I said, can I help you, boss?" Rich smiled and it transformed his face into something approaching the friendliness she was used to.

"Morning, Rich." Rowan mustered up a smile for him. "Have you seen Glen this morning?"

It worked. His own smile increased. "No, boss. He's out this week. You gave him the week off, remember?"

"Of course I do."

Rich raised an eyebrow.

"Okay, okay, I totally forgot."

"Good one." Rich laughed. "How did you and Glen make out at site?"

"It went all right. Site visits are *always* fun." Rowan shifted her briefcase into her other hand.

"At least they're not a feral customer."

Rowan nodded. "They were fine." *I hope.*

"Yeah. Ryan and Vic are both good guys."

No they're not. Rowan nodded. "Yep." She gestured toward her office. "Time to get my nose to the grindstone."

She turned before Rich could respond and disappeared into her office. She dropped her briefcase onto her desk with a sigh. The blotter had a few names and numbers on it. Her desk was bare of any personal items. *In this reality, I went to site with Glen. I think she's right. Something happened to her in this reality and she doesn't work for Octahedron. I'm kind of glad we're in the old office. I couldn't stand seeing her empty office. It'd kill me.* She smiled briefly. *I wonder if I approved his vacation. If I was planning on doing it when I got back that'd be good. It'd give me an excuse to go into the HR system and find his address.*

Rowan dragged out her laptop and slid it into the docking station. She booted it up with a sigh, praying that the day would pass quickly.

AFTER AN HOUR, Kelly pushed herself back from the desk. Her eyes stung and her head felt close to bursting with all the information she'd found.

She looked around the office. It almost felt like Rowan,

but not quite. She felt like she didn't belong in this Rowan's personal space.

Where the hell is the Rowan from this reality? Is she at work? Is my *Rowan okay?*

She picked up the cell phone Rowan had left her and swiped it. The keypad obediently swam into focus.

Do I want to call her? That's probably a bad idea. I don't want to come across as clingy. I can't help it. I want to wrap myself around her and not let go. I'm terrified and I can't express to her why. Oh, she knows it's because I'm scared because I don't exist in this world, but I wonder if she's really thought things all the way through to their logical conclusion? If anything happens to her, if she dies, *God forbid, my death will be minutes or hours later. I* can't *live here without her. And I don't* want *to live here without her either.*

She looked at the keyboard for a moment. *I could ask her to marry me—gay marriage is completely legal here—but we couldn't really get married. I don't have a birth certificate or anything here. God, I'm so fucked.*

She got up, feeling restless. "I'm going to take a bit of a poke around this little city."

She went back into the kitchen and pulled the keys to Rowan's company car off the hook, and the spare keys to the house. She automatically felt in her pocket for her wallet and shrugged. What did it matter whether or not she had her driver's license?

She left the house, locking the door behind her. She slipped behind the wheel of the car. Her eyes widened. "Wow."

The car parked in front of the company car was an immaculate EH Holden, painted a pale turquoise. The wide walkway along the side of the carport offered protection from the elements. This car looked as though it'd never seen rain, wet roads, or dust in its entire life.

Kelly backed out onto the road and slowly made her way toward Eastgardens. She reached Bunnerong Road, but instead of going into Eastgardens, she found herself following Bunnerong Road, around to Gardeners Road.

The houses here were old and sturdily built, but it still looked like they'd taken a beating. Some of the roofs where badly damaged and shattered tile lay on the ground around them; the curtains were dusty and torn in most cases; some of the windows were broken and the ones that weren't were filthy.

Kelly shivered. *God, this is horrible. This so feels like a dying world. I don't know how anyone could live here. How could anyone make a life here? There are some things that are incredibly attractive—like, the lack of homophobia and that Rowan and I could marry—but that hardly makes up for the other stuff. I feel like we're so far away from home we may as well be on another planet.*

She drove up Gardeners road toward her old block of flats. The road was lightly trafficked, unlike the way she normally knew it. She turned left down Sutherland Street, first right down Tramway lane, and all the way down to her unit.

The laneway was littered with rubble and potholes. The houses on either side looked as dirty and neglected as everything else. She felt shocked when she finally stopped at the back of her flat. The top two units were shattered wrecks and there was chain link fence around the back. It looked as though the units were going to be demolished.

Holy shit. I didn't like it all that much but it was home. Do I want to get out and look at where I used to live?

An image of Rowan's beautiful face flitted through her mind. *When we get back home, I'm going to make a life with Rowan. She's home. That's the same, no matter what reality I'm in. This . . . wreckage isn't home in any reality I'm familiar with.* She sighed and backed down the alleyway to the nearest intersection. She prayed there was no traffic as she backed out onto the road. It was deserted. She sighed with relief.

She headed back toward Rowan's—now *their*—house. As she turned back onto Bunnerong Road, she decided to go to La Perouse and watch the planes taking off from across Botany Bay.

She drove past the paper mill—in this world it was abandoned and the air smelt clean—and down toward La Perouse. The road stopped just past the cemetery. She stopped in front of a couple of barriers that announced that the road was closed.

"What the fuck?"

She got out of the car and went past the signs.

Jesus Christ.

A gigantic sink hole gouged the road in two. *Look how deep it is. That's wide. I couldn't walk around it even if I wanted to.*

She got back into the car with a sigh and flipped a neat turn.

She shuddered. *Fuck this. I give up. I want to go home.*

CHAPTER 17

ROWAN SAT AT her desk, staring out of the window. She was distantly grateful that all she could see was a shabby version of Central Station in the distance.

I'm glad I can't see the water. I wonder how Kelly's doing? She sighed. *I hate it here. I may have a life I can step into—it almost feels like shifting countries and already having a job lined up for yourself—but I don't belong here. I don't want to stay. I want to go home.*

She glanced at her door. She'd done a round of the technician's desks and had seen Glen's empty cube again. Her calendar told her that he wouldn't be back until Wednesday—he had a couple of days of vacation.

She scanned her e-mail. *I hope I didn't approve his vacation yet. Yes. There is. The notification that something requires my action.*

She logged into payroll and approved his vacation, and then quickly skipped over to his personal details. She grabbed a Post-it note and wrote down his address. It was in North Sydney. *Score. Kelly's going to be happy with this.*

Her smile slipped a little at the thought of Kelly. She could see from Kelly's unhappy demeanor that she was falling apart on the inside. *How am I ever going to get her to understand that it's her I want, not her earning potential or domestic skills?*

She remembered the feel of Kelly's soft lips and smooth skin, her breathless cries of passion. *I was always attracted to her. Now I know I'm in love with her. She's adaptable, strong, and sweet. She's incredibly intelligent and has a very practical way of looking at things.*

There was a knock at the door.

"Huh?" she said, looking up.

A short woman leant in the doorway. Her breasts threatened to tumble out of her shirt.

"Hi, Lisa." Rowan dredged up a smile. "How's HR world?"

Lisa strolled in. She sauntered around the back of the desk and before Rowan could react, planted a deep, wet kiss on her.

Rowan instantly pulled away, shocked. "Now, now. We're in the office."

"That's not what you said last time." Lisa grinned at her.

"I decided to develop standards?"

"Sure." Lisa laughed. "You busy tonight?"

Rowan nodded, thinking of Kelly. "Sorry."

"How about Friday?"

"I'll call you." Rowan smiled and hoped against hope they would be gone by Friday.

Lisa ran her finger down Rowan's chest and dipped it between her breasts. Rowan gaped at her.

"Later," Lisa said, sauntering back out of Rowan's office.

Rowan sank back in her chair feeling guilty and disgusted. *The desk is probably clear because other me's conquests keep knocking stuff off it.* "I'm such a *pig*. I'm *horrible* in this reality."

She picked up her cell phone and looked at it. Her fingers itched to dial Kelly's number. She gave into the urge.

The phone picked up after a couple of rings.

"Hi, Rowan," Kelly said. She sounded dejected.

"Hey, Kell. I missed you. What's wrong? You sound so sad."

"I miss you, too. I've spent most of my morning web surfing and I found some stuff."

"Anything you can tell me now?"

"Only that I was stillborn in this world. My mother lived and I died. In our reality it's the other way around."

"Do you want to go and see her?"

"I can't. She's dead."

"Oh, that's terrible, love. I'm sorry."

There was a long pause. "Thank you, love."

Rowan stared at her cell phone. Kelly sounded peculiar. "Are you at home?"

"Yeah." Kelly sighed.

"*Are* you all right, Kell?"

"Yeah, I'm fine."

"Do you want to meet me for lunch?"

"Thanks, love, but I have some stuff I want to do."

"Okay," Rowan said doubtfully.

"I love you. Give me a call when you're ready to be picked up."

"Okay. I love you. Bye."

"Bye."

The phone disconnected.

I'm going home. There's something wrong.

She opened up a messaging session to David.

KELLY WANTED TO go for a walk and clear her head. She felt as though she'd gone and stared into bedroom windows all morning long and seen things she hadn't wanted to see. She sat in the living room bent down, and laced her joggers.

She heard a car pull up outside the house.

"Now what? Who's that?" she mumbled, straightening.

Rowan got out of the front seat of the taxi and a tangled set of emotions washed over her, too quick to identify, followed by a terrible wave of longing.

Rowan jogged up the path and a few seconds later the door opened and she let herself in.

Kelly gazed at her, soaking in her beautiful features, and felt her heart do a slow flip flop.

Rowan dropped her briefcase in the foyer. "You sounded terrible. I got the rest of the week off and came home."

Suddenly Kelly was in Rowan's arms, squeezing her, loving the solid feel of her body pressed against the length of hers.

"I'm glad you're home. I needed you." Kelly felt the sting of tears.

Rowan's arms tightened around her. "What's wrong?" She pulled back and stared into Kelly's eyes. She wiped away Kelly's tears with gentle fingers. "Something's really bothering you. What?"

Kelly wanted to lie. She couldn't. "I went through the other *you*'s office today and I found stuff that I could easily have lived without seeing."

"Show me."

Kelly took Rowan's hand and led her into the office. She opened the filing cabinet drawer and silently took out the address book and the sheaf of bank statements.

Rowan looked at the bank statements. "This is real," she said, after scanning them for a few seconds. She looked at Kelly. "My reality is like this as well."

Kelly pushed the address book toward her and pulled out the framed pictures as Rowan scanned it.

"This isn't me, Kell." Rowan looked at Kelly, hurt lurking in her blue eyes. "You don't really think I'd do this to you, do you?"

Kelly remained silent.

"Oh, geez, Kell," Rowan said, a spark of anger in her blue eyes. "This isn't *me*. It's another version of me. I never walked down this road. And you know me pretty well by now. What on earth makes you think I'd be so awful to you? What did *I* do to deserve *this* lack of trust?"

Kelly caught her arm as she was walking out of the room. Rowan glanced down at her hand and her jaw clenched.

"More," Kelly said. "And this one I *do* want to know about. And I *need* to talk about this."

Rowan gave her a sharp nod.

Kelly pushed the picture of Rowan and Karen toward her.

Rowan's eyes widened. "Wow. I haven't thought about her in years."

"Who is she?"

Rowan sighed. "When I was in university, I'd figured out I was a lesbian and I was trying to work out how that fit in my life." She snorted. "My family was a little bit homophobic. I'm glad they're over that now. Karen was the first woman I ever slept with. We were together for a year and were crazy about each other. She was a year ahead of me and at the end of her final year she got a job offer overseas. It was me or the job and the job won. We loved each other but it just wasn't right, you know?"

Kelly nodded. "I get that."

"Looks like she stayed here in this reality." Rowan put down the picture. "What do you want to talk about?"

"Let's go for a walk."

KELLY SHIVERED AND pulled in closer to Rowan. Rowan slipped her arm around her shoulders.

"It's cold out here," Kelly said.

They walked down toward a park on a bluff overlooking the ocean. The purple sky was almost completely covered with greenish grey clouds. They passed houses, half of which looked abandoned, the other half simply empty for the day.

The traffic was light as they crossed the road and went into the park. Parts of it were chained off. Behind the chains were tall plants that almost looked like mutant sunflowers. They turned as they approached, as though watching them, alien and unknowable.

Kelly pulled Rowan over to a bench close to the edge of a grassy cliff. Wind rushed over and around them and in the distance the poisonous ocean was whipped into a frenzy by it.

"You want to know about the address book, don't you?" Rowan asked. She felt sick thinking about it.

"Yes," Kelly said, turning and looking at her.

"I don't know who most of those women are," Rowan said. "I think this me slept her way through the entire lesbian population in Sydney."

"I don't like it."

"Neither do I." Rowan sighed. "*I'm* not like that. I was a bit wilder when I was in my twenties and I freely admit to liking sex but I'm not promiscuous."

Kelly remained silent, studying her. Something flickered in her eyes.

"You remember when I said I was single but I was taken?"

Kelly nodded after a moment.

"I didn't have a steady lover and I didn't want one." She felt her face heat. "I haven't wanted one for a few years." She smiled and steeled herself. "It started when I interviewed you. You were beautiful, elegant, and intelligent. You knew what you were doing. I liked that. Then we began working together and I realized you were always cool, you never lost your temper, you were fair, sweet, and funny. I liked being around you. Then I started to realize I wanted you. That never passed. It got worse. I found that I *wanted* to be around you. I loved it when we went to lunch together. I kept my hands to myself because I thought you were straight. And even if you weren't, I never thought you'd be interested in me." She was silent a moment, studying Kelly's beautiful features. "I finally have my chance with you and I want to make a real go of it. I'd hate to think it was ruined because of things *I've* never done."

Kelly nodded. She took a deep breath. "I was always attracted to you as well. I never let it get any further than that because I was in a relationship. Letting myself feel more for you would have put me on a path to destruction. I loved having you as my boss. I loved it when we spent time together outside the office. I was so happy when we *finally* got to go on a business trip together. It was kind of like Christmas for me, you know?"

Rowan smiled at that.

Kelly's voice dropped to almost a whisper. "I'm so sorry, but I'm a mess. I'm afraid that we're not going to get home. I have no way of contributing to *us* outside of being a housewife and I'm not geared up to be that. That's not me. But there's so much other stuff. If I get sick, I can't go to a doctor. I can't get a job. I can't drive. All of that terrifies me." She sounded like she was forcing out the words.

It hurt Rowan to hear the insecurity from her. "I understand, Kelly."

Kelly nodded. "The thing that makes it really bad for me is that I know Genevieve has cheated on me more than once. I think I've always turned a blind eye to it because it meant that I was free from her for even a brief period of time." She looked straight at Rowan. "You're so beautiful. I'm sure women hit on you all the time." She blushed. "I'm the jealous type. I don't like sharing. I can't stand the thought of you in another woman's arms. *I* want to be the one you come home to. *I* want to be the one you talk to in the middle of the night when all the demons come out. *I* want to be *the one* for you."

Rowan pulled her in close. Kelly encircled her with her arms and squeezed her. She rested her chin on Kelly's head and gave her a gentle kiss. "You're already all of those things. I won't hurt you, Kelly. I promise." She tilted up Kelly's face so they could see each other's eyes. "I'm *not* a cheat. We're *not* staying here. We're an *us*. Where you go, I go. *My* life isn't really worth living without you either. *We* will work this out. *We* are going home."

"What if we don't remember any of this when we get home?"

"I'm going to make a move on you. You're my lover. I have you now and I'm not willing to let go either." She wiped away Kelly's tears. "*I* don't like to share either. And it upsets me to think of any other woman touching *you* like I do. I *want* you to stay mine. I *want* to work on us."

Kelly nodded and they were comfortably silent for a moment.

"Besides snooping, I did web surfing this morning as well," Kelly said.

"Oh," Rowan said. "Before you tell me about it. I forgot. I looked up Glen this morning and found his address. We should go looking for him."

"Nice one. I think we're probably going to have to go looking for him tomorrow morning."

"Why don't we go this afternoon?"

"Because it's going to rain and that's a bad thing," Kelly said. "The rain here is toxic. That's why you have a covered walkway from the carport to the house. That's also why the roof on your house is so thick. It's to keep out the rain."

Rowan wasn't sure she wanted to know. "That sounds ominous."

"It is. About twenty years ago, there was a shower of meteors that came through the atmosphere. They have a peculiar kind of radiation in them. It's toxic to life here. It made people sick and they died. It killed off almost all of the vegetation. The authorities realized almost as soon as the meteor showers started but there wasn't the infrastructure in place to be able to save lives. About fifty percent of life died before adequate shelters were in place to save the other fifty percent. Not that it mattered anyway. Prolonged exposure to the radiation makes you sterile. *Prolonged* means months. Now that science has finally figured all of that out, humanity is starting to regroup. That's why civilization hasn't fallen apart completely yet."

Rowan felt sick.

Kelly looked up at the sky. "We should head back to the house. We don't want to be outside when it rains." She tugged at her shirt. "Lucky we both wore stuff that's in your wardrobe. Apparently fashion now incorporates some measure of radiation shielding. Won't help us much against the rain, though."

Rowan looked up. The sky had gotten darker and more threatening. She stood, pulling Kelly with her. She took Kelly's hand and they walked back to the house.

Kelly squeezed her hand and snuggled into her. "Society has shifted here completely. It's legal for us to get married. Religion collapsed completely so you'll find few, if any, churches in use here."

"That explains why the cathedral in the middle of town looks like a wreck. No one cares about it anymore."

"And as a result, society's flourished because of it. Well, what's left of it anyway."

"Now that we've covered all of the boring stuff, what did you find out about yourself?"

"Mostly what I told you already. I was stillborn. My father's gone too, but no surprises there. He died of cancer here like he did there. I know where both of them are buried."

"Do you want to go and visit their graves?"

Kelly shook her head. "They're both buried in Melbourne."

"Ah. No, side trip isn't that good an idea." Rowan looked at Kelly. "How did you find out all of that stuff, anyway? I thought most of it would be information you wouldn't have easy access to."

"I don't know why but hacking's not as prevalent here as it is in our reality. Computers must not be the same here. Either way, the privacy laws are much looser and these guys have something called a *Freedom to Obtain Information Act.* It allows you to get a lot more information here that's off limits to us."

"So this world really would be paradise for us if we could stay."

"It would be the Garden of Eden if it wasn't for the fact that this earth is poisoned."

They heard a crack of thunder in the distance. They were a couple of blocks from the house and they began jogging. They quickly reached the house and let themselves in. The heavens opened and glowing, greenish yellow rain came down from the sky in solid sheets. Rowan watched it from the front windows and felt sick.

Kelly slipped her arms around Rowan's waist.

"Forget the rain. We're safe. Forget Glen for a while. I need you. I need to *be* with you," Kelly whispered.

Rowan turned in the circle of her arms. The distortion of the rain against the thick glass cast sharp angles and jagged plains on Kelly's beautiful face. Her dark eyes showed her pain and fear, warring uneasily with her desire.

"I love you, Kell," Rowan whispered as Kelly led her into the bedroom.

CHAPTER 18

IT WAS FULL night by the time the rain stopped.

Rowan, dressed in her robe, opened the front door. Damp air with an acrid undertone of rotting fish flowed into the house. She quickly closed the door.

That explains the terrible smell. I thought it was just dying vegetation.

Kelly, wearing her spare robe, was in the kitchen, rifling through the cupboards for something other than canned ravioli or spaghetti. Rowan sat down on one of the kitchen chairs and watched her.

We're going home. I promise. *I don't know how much of this I'll remember but I can't imagine forgetting you or forgetting that you're* the one *for me. God, how could* anyone *cheat on you? You're the most amazing woman I've ever met. You're easily the best lover I've had. I can't imagine wanting anyone else as close to me as you are.*

"Penny for your thoughts," Kelly said as she turned around. She was holding a can. Her eyes darkened at the sight of Rowan. "Close your robe, love. If you don't, *you're* going to become dinner."

Rowan felt like wagging her tail. She grinned and pulled her robe closed. "What did you find there?"

"Oh," Kelly said. She looked at the can. "Chinese."

"This should be interesting." Rowan snorted a laugh. "I haven't had that since I was in uni."

Kelly shrugged. "Beats canned Italian."

"Wonder if we can get canned Indian?"

"Probably."

Kelly opened the can and dumped the contents into a pot. "Well? Are you going to tell me what's going through your mind?"

You. "I was wondering if you wanted to go to Glen's place after we had a bite?"

"Has the rain stopped?"

"Yeah. Smells bad out there but not enough to turn your stomach."

"If that's not a sparkling recommendation, I don't know what is."

Rowan shrugged. "This place sucks no matter how you slice it."

"Where does this Glen live?"

"North Sydney."

"You want to take the company car?"

"Nope. I think he's used it too often. He'll spot it a mile away. We can easily sneak up on him if we take my car."

"Not that gorgeous EH Holden station wagon?"

"That one."

"Can I drive? I love that car."

"Sure."

Kelly comfortably settled herself onto Rowan's lap. She stole a kiss. "Do you have one of those in our reality?"

Rowan nodded. "Yep. That was my dad's car. He gave it to me when I graduated from uni. I fixed it up over the course of a few years and now it's my main buddy on the weekends." She nodded toward the stove. "I think that's ready."

Kelly reluctantly got off her lap. A few moments later they cautiously tasted their food.

"Tastes canned," Rowan said.

"Yeah." Kelly nodded. "Okay. So what's the plan of attack with Glen?"

"We're going to go and see if he's there. If he is, we're going to find out *which* Glen he is. Fatigues Glen or Purple Sky World Glen."

"Purple sky world Glen? I like that." Kelly took a bite of her food and shrugged. "Fair." She took another bite. "I've been wondering on and off what happened to this world's Rowan."

"I'm guessing that Rowan has shifted realities as well. I don't know where she would have ended up."

Kelly was silent a moment. "This is so weird. I mean I was always familiar with the idea of multiple universes but I never thought it was *real*."

"I know," Rowan said. "And actually, if you think about it, we don't know that if we shift realities again we're going to end up in our own reality. We could easily end up in a different one."

"Sometimes you just gotta roll the dice, love."

"And hope it doesn't end up the way it did here? I just want us *both* to have lives in whatever world we finally land in."

"I wonder what would happen to us if we stayed here?"

"I honestly don't know. Think about it. Every second a new reality peels off from the one you're in. In one reality I finished my food. In another one, I didn't. What would be the consequences of that? In the long run, it doesn't matter. What matters is that I'm split into two and one is hungry later, the other isn't. But both versions of *me* don't belong in this reality."

Kelly shook her head. "It hurts thinking about it."

"What I don't understand is *how* someone managed to do this. I read a theoretical physics book once that said the energy requirements were more than the total amount of energy in the universe."

"That was the universe we came from, right? How do you know that wasn't a simple one to solve in a *different* reality?"

"I don't but I see that it's a distinct possibility." Rowan was silent a moment, allowing her mind to shoot through a myriad of outcomes. "Either way, you still come back to the question of *why* someone would want to do this."

"Being a movie buff, the first thing plot dictates is that *they* were trying to change something or escape something."

"Perfectly logical and reasonable."

"And it hurts my head."

They laughed.

Rowan glanced at the kitchen clock. It was eight. "Let's clean up and get moving, yes?"

Kelly nodded, taking Rowan's bowl. "Works for me." She set the bowls in the sink and ran water into them.

"Stuff the dishes, love," Rowan said with a grin.

Kelly laughed. "Sorry, force of habit."

Rowan took her hand and led her into the bedroom.

CHAPTER 19

"THIS IS THE place?" Rowan asked as Kelly pulled up outside a massive block of units in North Sydney. The acrid stench of Sydney Harbor drifted in waves through the car's open windows. Kelly had to control her gag reflex.

"This is it." Kelly studied Rowan's perfect profile. "Are you ready?"

Rowan twisted around and grabbed something off the floor behind the driver's seat.

"A *softball* bat?" Kelly asked. "You really think that's going to be necessary?"

"I don't know," Rowan said. "I don't want to leave anything to chance."

She's right. I couldn't stand it if she got hurt. Softball bat comes.

"Let's do this, then," Kelly said. "I don't want to be caught on the road or outside if it starts to rain again."

Rowan nodded. "Neither do I."

They got out of the car and dodged light traffic as they jogged across the road.

Kelly experimentally tried the front door. It opened easily.

"I was expecting it to be a security door," Rowan said.

"I didn't know what to expect," Kelly said. "This place is just plain, fucking weird."

Rowan snorted a laugh and nodded.

"Stairs or lift?" Kelly asked.

"His flat number is ten eighteen. Lift. You really want to walk up ten flights of stairs and probably get into a fight with him?"

"While I would normally consider that a good workout, in this case I think I'll suspend my exercise ethic."

Rowan gaped at her and after a second or so burst out laughing. "Thanks, love. I needed that."

Kelly smiled. "Here to help." She pressed the call car button.

They waited for a few moments and the shabby lift doors opened. They got into a lift that looked as though it'd seen too much use. The doors wheezed closed and they jolted into motion.

"The lift stinks." Rowan wrinkled her nose.

"I'll bet the lift shaft is leaking."

"Probably."

The lift slid to a halt on the tenth floor. They got out and Kelly pulled Rowan to a halt just before ten eighteen.

"What's the plan?"

Rowan hefted the bat. "We'll knock and try to have a civil conversation with him. If he's not interested, we'll persuade him. *If* it's Mr. Fatigues."

"Okay," Kelly said. *That's the grand plan? We're fucked.* "Ready?" Rowan nodded.

Kelly knocked on the door.

The door slid open a couple of inches and Glen's wary features appeared in the gap. He looked at her for a second or so. His eyes widened and his features twisted into a look of pure terror. He scrabbled back, and Kelly stepped through the widening gap in the doorway.

She glanced at Rowan who looked as surprised as she felt.

"God, no." Glen moaned. "Don't hurt me, Colonel."

Kelly gaped at him. *Colonel?*

"Get up, Glen," Rowan said. "No one's here to hurt you."

"Who the hell do you think I am?" Kelly asked.

Glen's eyes narrowed in suspicion. "Colonel Kelly Carne. Commander in Chief of the State Police."

"Bzzzt. Wrong. I'm Kelly Carne but I'm not the commander in chief of anything." She took a step closer to him and he took a step back. "As far as I know, this place doesn't *have* a State Police. If it does, it's certainly not what you're thinking, whatever that may be."

"You're not from here, are you, Glen? Well, neither are we. We want to go home and I think you can help us with that," Rowan said smoothly. She held the bat in her hand, seemingly relaxed but ready to move quickly.

Glen eyed them both. He shook his head.

"Where *are* you from?"

"Someplace else. Just like you," he said. His shoulders slumped. "Who are you?"

Kelly took in his buzz cut and the twisted scar running down one side of his rugged features. "That's Rowan May. I'm Kelly Carne. In another reality, you work for both of us. You're a senior software technical analyst."

"And you're one in this world as well. You work for me, here." Rowan tilted her head and studied him. "You seem to know about reality jumping, don't you?"

Glen nodded warily.

"Which reality are you from? It's not ours, we know that. We're looking for *our* Glen. Did you do something to him, soldier?"

Glen went pale.

"We found your fatigues in Settler's Creek Motel," Kelly said. "And Glen's cell phone. They *were* your fatigues, weren't they?"

Glen gave her a sharp nod. He tensed, as though ready to spring, and Rowan gripped the bat tighter.

Why the hell isn't he fighting us? He's bigger than either one of us. We'd probably lose a scuffle with him. He's not resisting. This doesn't make sense. Why?

Kelly took a step toward him and he took a step backward.

"Why are you so frightened of me?" Kelly asked.

Glen remained silent. He tensed and moved so quickly that Kelly was caught off guard. He lunged toward her, his face twisted in a snarl of rage.

Rowan wasn't surprised. She moved as soon as he did, jabbing him in the stomach with the end of the bat. The air left his lungs in a sharp grunt. Rowan kicked him as hard as she could and he collapsed like a stone, clutching his battered manhood.

Rowan bent down on one knee and looked him in the eye. "I have five older brothers. Don't try anything. Do you think we could talk calmly for a few minutes?"

Glen moaned and struggled to his feet. He collapsed on the couch.

"You got quite a punch," he said.

"Can we talk for a few minutes without it turning into combat?"

Glen nodded.

"Who are you and where are you from?"

"My name is Sergeant Glen Adams. I'm in the World Army."

"Okay, Sergeant Adams from the World Army. Where are you from?"

"I come from a dying world. I don't want to go back and you can't make me."

"We're not here to *make* you do anything besides tell us where *our* Glen is," Kelly cut in.

Rowan nodded. "How did you shift realities?"

Glen blew out a lung full of air. "The Science Division built an Ark. I wasn't chosen and I didn't want to die so I left."

"So you're saying your reality's experiment threw us out of our world?"

"If you were in the bubble when they turned on the generator, yes."

"We weren't in your reality when they powered up the generator," Kelly said. "How could we have been caught in the bubble?"

"I don't know. I don't understand science stuff. I'm not smart enough for the science corps. I'm dumb, I always was. All I know is that I don't want to be fodder for a dying world." Glen gave them both an uneasy look. "Are you going to send me back?"

"Do you really want to stay here? In a dying world?" Rowan asked.

"Compared to where I'm from, this is paradise. *Yes* I want to stay here."

"Why?" Kelly asked. "Why would you want to stay in such a poisonous, desolate place?"

Glen shook his head. "You've never seen my world. It's full of people who believe in God. We live by God's law. Everything they do is in God's name. They decided to remove sin from the world so they built a eugenics program. They build a smarter population with all the same vices and weaknesses that we're all prone to. But somehow they twist it around so it's the fault of those who *weren't* the result of the eugenics program. They decide they're going to leave to find Eden. They love us, you see, and are doing it for our own good. Our corruption is made worse by their perfection and devotion to Jesus. They don't want to be part of the rapture since they don't deserve it, being the next evolution of mankind. Love the sinner and hate the sin, they say." He gave a small, bitter smile. "So they build an Ark so they can move to a perfect place where there is no sin. In the meantime, they tear apart the fabric of reality for the rest of us. For them, it becomes evidence for the impending rapture and they speed up their experiments and timeline. It's a vicious circle but it doesn't matter. The bottom line is that my world is ending. I don't want to be part of that. I'll take my chances here, thanks. I'll stick with people who don't treat me like a moronic freak because I'm just a dumb guard at a government facility."

Kelly felt sick. *If he's telling the truth it's no wonder that he doesn't want to go back.*

Rowan was silent a moment. "Did you do something to our Glen?"

Glen was silent for a few moments. "Are you going to send me back?"

Rowan and Kelly exchanged a long look.

I don't understand this guy at all. He's totally unlike any man I've ever met. He should have dragged out his macho at least once by now. But he's not. He's like a frightened child. And he's terrified of me.

"Glen," Kelly said. "Are you going to help us?"

"Only if you don't send me back."

"I'm not sure how you think we *could* send you back," Rowan said. "So I'd say you've answered your own question."

"I know you can't send me back," Glen said.

"Then why do you keep asking?"

"I want to see you answer."

"Then no, we aren't going to send you back."

Kelly gave Rowan a sharp look.

Rowan gave her a rueful smile. "We couldn't even if we wanted to. None of us are holding the cards here. He's not in a position to push us around and we're not in a position to push *him* around."

"He doesn't belong here any more than we do."

"Maybe not. But same question that plagues us plagues him as well. Where's the Glen from this world? Where's the Rowan from this world? Where did they go? Do *they* want to come home?" Rowan paused and looked at her carefully. "If you actually existed in this world, would you want to leave it? *We* could have a future here. This world would be ideal for *us* if it wasn't a toxic, dying world."

I see her point. If I existed, we could be married. We could probably have children. We'd have a life. But I'm dead here. We don't have families here. We have *to go home, even though it's not ideal, for us to be* really *together the way things should be. I'd say that's the major reason we* both *want to leave.*

"No," Kelly said to Glen. "We *won't* send you back. Even if we could, we wouldn't do it." She studied Glen. "You should tell us more about this experiment and Ark of yours."

Glen closed his eyes and took a deep breath. "I'll talk. I'll tell more." He gestured toward the recliners. "Take a seat."

Rowan and Kelly sank into the chairs opposite him.

"I come from a dying world. There is an Ark. Only the genetically perfect were selected to go on it. I was one of the guards for the Ark. They were going to do five power ups of the Ark over the course of ten days. It takes a full twenty four hours for the generator to power up again once it's been used. When they ran their first experiment, I watched to see how to turn on and steer the Ark. They powered up for the first time and sent a test pilot to what they thought was another world. He came back after a few seconds. He said he'd seen a fire pit and a swag man. From his description, it sounded like the memorial fire pit at the end of the road past Department of Defense." He smiled without humor. "I know it well. I spent a lot of time getting drunk with my friends there before they were all arrested and executed, one by one.

"Anyway, the swag man was so frightened of him that he fell into his own fire and burned to death. That didn't sound like it was a new world to me, it just sounded like someplace else. I got curious about it. I began thinking. Some of the stuff I'd overheard began to make sense. The lab coats kept talking about alternate realities. I decided to do my own kind of research and looked for anything I could find about the history of that place. There *was* no fire at the fire pit. There *was* a swag man. He was on his way to Ithaca to visit family and stayed there overnight. Legend has it he'd seen something. A man in a silver suit. Of course, everyone there at the time thought he was insane and his family took him in to take care of him. Despite being considered psychotic, he was regarded as a brilliant business man and went on to end up owning almost all of the land from Settler's Creek to Ithaca. He went on to become an influential politician in Queensland and then on to become the Prime Minister. He was regarded as an all-round good, God fearing man, the father of our modern world.

"I asked the pilot about what he'd seen. He said the swag man fell into the bush and started up a fire, but the pilot didn't know anymore because he snapped back to our reality. I thought about it. If all of that was true, it meant that our reality split off into alternate realities from there. In one reality, the swag man survived. In another, he caught fire and fell down one side of the ridge and burned one town. In another, he fell down the *other* side of the ridge and burned the *other* town. I saw I had a way out. I didn't *have* to stay put in my world. I could *leave*. There *were* places I could go where I could survive. In those places, the Ark had never been built and it didn't tear apart the fabric of our world. I didn't have to die. *That* sounded appealing to me. I needed help so I told some of my friends. The ones who were still alive, that is. I was on the night shift, so I waited until the place was empty. The generator was at full power so we took our chances."

"Who's *we*?" Kelly asked.

"Richards, Brenton, and Sanders."

"Where are they all now?"

"I don't know. We got separated. I think they may have been caught. We broke through into another reality but things snapped back overnight. It was like a ripple effect. I hid overnight but must have gone to sleep. I woke up in this reality and ran like hell to get out of the bubble. I did some research on the history of this world and it's not the same one I left. No one seems to have come looking for me. If they did, they haven't found me. I don't think they know where to look for me and I don't know they care all that much. One missing dummy like me? Not enough to waste energy or manpower on. I'd like it to stay that way."

Rowan chewed her lip. "So that means that if they stick to their regular schedule, they should be retrying their experiment tomorrow night. Right?"

Glen nodded. "Right."

"We just have to be in the bubble to shift realities, don't we?"

"Yes. It's that simple."

"Kell, let's go. We don't have a lot of time to get there."

Kelly looked at Rowan's watch. It was almost nine. That meant that they would be in Settler's Creek at six the following evening if they began driving now.

"Can I talk to you alone for a moment, Rowan?" Kelly looked pointedly at Glen.

Glen stood up. "I'll give you some space." He reached into his pocket and pulled out a packet of cigarettes. He disappeared out onto the balcony.

"What the fuck, Rowan?"

Rowan smiled. "None of this matters. What he wants doesn't matter. You and I have to go home. That's the bottom line after you cut away all of the bullshit."

"What if he's lying to us?"

"How could things get any worse than they are now? So what if he's lying? The bubble he's talking about gels with what we experienced while we were in Settler's Creek. So that part is probably the truth. If we go up there then we stand a good chance of going home. You want to take it?"

She's right. This is surreal. It doesn't make any sense.

Something's wrong here. "Say he's telling us the full truth. What happens if we're walking into some kind of trap?"

"Again, what does it matter? No matter what, we can't stay here."

"You're right." Kelly threw up her hands. "But for what it's worth, I don't trust him. At all."

Rowan studied her. "I don't either. But I also don't see what options we have here."

"Out of curiosity, why do you think he's so eager to get rid of us?"

"I have no idea." Rowan took Kelly's hand and caressed it. "Sometimes you just gotta jump and trust your luck."

"All right," Kelly said. "Let's just go."

Rowan nodded. "Glen?"

Glen stubbed out his cigarette and came back into the living room.

"We're going," Rowan said. "Good luck here."

"You promise not to tell them where I am?"

"I promise to keep my mouth shut if they ask me, whoever *they* may be."

"Thank you," Glen said.

"I don't get it, Glen," Kelly said. "You're not trying to fight us. You seem to be telling the truth. Why?"

Glen studied them for a minute. "If I go back there, they'll kill me. It'll be the firing squad. If I stay here the radiation will kill me. You aren't from this reality and if your Glen was anything to go by, yours is better than this reality or my home. I understand why you want to go back. Bottom line—I don't want my life there anymore. I'd try and fight you if you wanted to take me back. I don't want to hurt anyone. I just want to live here. I'll kill anyone from my world who comes after me. I have a fifty-fifty chance that you won't end up in *my* reality; you could end up in your own. If you go back there, no harm done to any of us."

Kelly nodded. *It still doesn't make any sense to me.*

ROWAN STARTED THE engine with a sigh. "That was very unsatisfying."

"Yeah, it was. I don't understand him at all."

Rowan did a quick U turn, praying that there weren't any police to see it. "I think he's lost hope. And he knows he screwed us."

"That can't be all."

"Isn't that enough? Have you really explored what's happening to us?"

"What do you mean?"

"Every action has a multitude of consequences. You know that, right?"

"Of course."

"Okay, then. Hear me out."

She felt Kelly studying her profile. The Pacific Highway stretched out ahead of them, lightly trafficked and dimly lit.

"Every second we live, another reality peels away from us. He had a choice in the reality he came from. If he hadn't powered up the machine again, he'd still be there and we might have been able to escape from Settler's Creek unscathed."

Kelly's eyes flashed. "So when Glen went nuts at site, that was the first experiment. When *we* came through they were probably out looking for him."

"In one reality, he stayed there. In another one, he left. In a different reality, he slipped through somewhere else. I'm sure there were a million combinations of destinations he could have chosen, but he got *our* reality. He could have left a moment sooner or a moment later. You know the probability of us just happening to run into *this* experiment at Settler's Creek was really, really low? We got badly unlucky. So did *our* Glen."

"Why the fuck does my fate have to be in someone else's hands?" Kelly snarled.

Rowan pulled into a brilliantly lit petrol station and fueled up the car. She looked up at the sky. It was pitch black with a carpet of stars she hadn't seen before. It was beautiful.

Wonder how long it takes for her to realize that the chances of us getting home to exactly where we belong is vanishingly low?

She replaced the nozzle and tank cap with a sigh. *No matter where we go, unless it's at exactly our starting point, we aren't going to belong. I feel like a refugee. And if what Glen said is true, then the people he works for are the most arrogant bastards on the face of any planet. Who are they to decide who's* genetically perfect *and that they can take over someone else's home?*

"Let me know when you want a rest," Kelly said. "I'm going to get some shut eye."

Rowan leaned over and kissed her, gently and sweetly. She felt like her life was spinning out of control. She *hated* how helpless she felt. She *hated* that her life felt like it was temporary. She *hated* feeling as though what she had no future with Kelly.

"What was that for?" Kelly asked breathlessly when they broke.

"To let you know I love you. Now and always. No matter what."

Kelly looked sad. She gently stroked Rowan's face. "I love you too."

Rowan pulled out onto the highway, feeling cold and lonely.

CHAPTER 20

"WAKE UP, LOVE," Rowan said.

Kelly's head ached and her eyes felt gritty as she finally got them open. "How long have I been asleep for?"

"About three hours," Rowan said. "I have to get out and stretch my legs."

Kelly looked around, blinking. They were in a truck stop by the side of the highway. Behind the service station and convenience store was a huge, dusty parking lot. They were parked close to the toilet. There were other cars parked a short distance away from them and trucks at the edges of the lot, all with their lights off and some with their engines on.

"Where are we?" she asked as the dome light flashed on.

Rowan was standing outside and stretching with a grimace. "I can't remember what this town is called but it's a couple of hours north of Newcastle."

Kelly got out and clutched the door as a wave of dizziness swept over her. She felt Rowan's hand on her back.

"Hey, Kell, are you all right?"

Kelly nodded. "Fine. It's just the normal blood rushing to my head thing."

Rowan kissed her temple. "All right. I'm going to go inside and see if I can pick us up something to eat. And something caffeinated if I can manage it."

"Ugh. Koff. Okay, if you get that stuff can I get what passes for milk and sugar in it in mine? Lots of it."

Rowan grinned. "You got it." She disappeared into the shadows around the front of the store.

Kelly watched her retreating back and wanted to cry. *I wish I could stay here. I'd ask her to marry me. I started this with her because I wanted her. Now I know I need her too. I'm scared.*

What if something happens to her? What happens if we somehow get split up?

She forced the thoughts back. They hurt too much. She felt moisture on her face and dimly realized she was crying.

She's what I want. What if I can't have her?

"Hey, hey, hey," Rowan said. She put two steaming Styrofoam cups on the bonnet of the car, and a couple of white paper bags. She slipped her arms around Kelly and pulled her in close. "What's the matter, love?"

Kelly took in her familiar scent and the warmth from her long, lean body and cried in earnest. She couldn't speak. Rowan held her, gently tracing patterns on her back and rocking her back and forth until the worst of her misery passed.

"I'm sorry, Rowan." Kelly pulled back and looked at Rowan's face, trying to commit every line to memory. "I'm just tense, that's all."

Rowan held her gaze. "That's not all of it, is it? What's the rest?"

Kelly held all of her courage in her hands and gave herself to Rowan. "I'm scared. What happens if we somehow don't both end up in the same reality?"

Rowan's grip tightened. "No matter what, Kelly, we're staying together. No matter what happens, I'm going to stay with you. I won't let us get split apart. I promise you."

Kelly snuggled into her, struggling against lingering doubt. "I promise you the same thing."

"Good." Rowan handed Kelly a hot drink. "Try that."

Kelly cautiously sipped it. It was still bitter but more palatable than the first time they'd tried it. "Either this stuff is growing on me or that's much better than last time."

"I think it's a combination of both. Try this. I got this, too. I thought you might like it."

Kelly pulled open the white bag. There was something in it that looked like some kind of pastry. She tore off a small corner and cautiously put it in her mouth. She tasted banana and flaky pastry. "Wow, that's not bad."

Rowan bit into hers. "No," she said around a mouth full of food. "Not bad at all."

"Should I ask what it's made of?"

Rowan shook her head. "That would be a bad idea."

They leaned against the car, looking up at the alien night sky, comfortably silent.

When they were done, they got in the car, Kelly behind the wheel, and began driving.

THEY WERE ON the outskirts of Brisbane by six in the morning. The traffic up the Pacific Freeway was light and fast moving. Rowan, taking her turn behind the wheel, sped through Brisbane as quickly as she could.

I don't care if I get hit by a speed camera. All I care about is getting up to Settler's Creek.

She glanced at Kelly, fast asleep in the passenger seat. She looked so *young*, her elegant features stripped of maturity as she slept. *I have to stop on the other side of the Gateway Bridge. I'm hungry. I need a bite to eat.*

She pulled up into a road stop just past the airport—and it sounded like there were planes in the air this morning—and Kelly started awake. She sat up and rubbed her eyes.

"Hey," she said, blinking. "What time is it?"

"It's about six thirty. I have to fill her up and I need a bite to eat."

Rowan got out of the car and began to fuel up. She yawned.

Kelly touched her arm. "Looks like there's a McDonalds in there." She blushed. "Can I borrow your debit card?"

Rowan smiled. "You're cute when you blush. And there's no need to be embarrassed around me, love." She reached into her jacket pocket and pulled out a wad of cash. "Here, use this. May as well since it's going to be monopoly money by tomorrow morning."

"Thanks. I hope."

"You hope thanks?"

Kelly grinned as she walked off. "No. I *hope* it's monopoly money by tomorrow morning."

"I hear you."

Rowan looked up at the sky. There was a border of dark grey cloud on the horizon. *Aw, shit. That's not good.* Another *meteor shower?*

She leant into the driver's side window and flicked on the radio. She surfed through the static until she found news radio. The announcer began a weather report. She listened carefully.

"Hey," Kelly said, leaning in the driver's side window. "Did you fall asleep?"

"No," Rowan said. "There's another meteor storm coming. Will probably hit us around five."

Kelly looked dismayed. "Oh, hell." She glanced at Rowan's watch. "If we push it we should be in Ithaca or Settler's Creek by the time it hits."

Rowan began to open the car door, but Kelly put her hands on it. We're ready to go. I already took care of the bowser and the petrol cap."

Rowan grinned and slid over into the passenger seat. "Thanks, darlin'."

"No worries, love." Kelly slid into the seat behind the steering wheel. "Now let's get to Rockie."

THEY WERE IN Rockhampton by twelve. Clouds moved swiftly across the sky, dulling the sunlight. There was an air of urgency as they slowly drove through Rockhampton.

"Do you want to do the honors and get us a bite to eat?" Rowan asked as they pulled over into another petrol station to fill up.

"Probably not a bad idea. Something light." Kelly grinned. "Like I could get anything else."

Rowan laughed.

Kelly went into the convenience store.

Rowan filled up, distantly pleased that the price of petrol was half what she was used to. She looked up at the sky. *God, it looks like it's going to rain. Can we be on the road when it rains?*

The wind picked up and the acrid stench of turning fish flowed over her in foul waves. She wrinkled her nose. *Why did it have to be rotting fish?*

Kelly jogged out of the convenience store, holding a small bag with what looked like grease stains on it and a couple of bottles of water.

"We have to get moving," she said without preamble. "Rain's expected. You have to have something special on your car to drive through it." She eyed the dusty EH. "You reckon this pretty lady might be outfitted for rain?"

"If it'd been up to me, I'd have done it as a precaution. If I really *had* to drive around, I'd have done it in my company car." She patted the EH's roof. "This is my baby. Let's run from the rain."

She got into the car behind the wheel.

"You want me to drive? You've done an awful lot today."

"I'm fine. Let's just get the hell out of here."

Kelly nodded and they pulled out of the service station and headed toward the Capricorn Highway. The traffic was light and they reached the fork quickly. Rowan munched on what she supposed was meant to be a hamburger.

"This isn't bad, Kell. What is it?"

Kelly grinned. "It's a hamburger," she said around a mouth full of food. "I like it. I'm not going to ask what it's made of. I haven't seen any cows."

Rowan laughed. "No. No bessies around here, that's for sure." She glanced in the rear view mirror and saw a yellow mist behind them. *Rain.*

She increased her speed.

The highway was as empty as it'd been when they drove up to Settler's Creek. They reached the turn off and Rowan found that her spirits were much better than they'd been for the past few days.

"I'm feeling better," Kelly said. "We're actually *doing*

something about going home. Not that we weren't but we have an answer on whether or not reality's going to shift. *Yes.*"

Rowan nodded. "I know. I'm already feeling more relaxed."

They made it halfway up the ridge. Rowan glanced at her watch. It was close to four.

"I need to pull over and stretch my legs," she said, driving into the rest stop opposite to the place she remembered it being.

"Oh, I could use a break." Kelly looked up at the sky. "Not long, though."

Rowan got out of the car and stretched out her back with a grimace. She slowly walked over to the monument set into an alcove on the cliff face.

> *Settler's Creek, June 20th, 1902*
> *Here, on this hill and in this valley, lie the remains of the one hundred and twelve souls of Settler's Creek. May they rest in peace.*

"Wow," Kelly said from directly beside her.

Rowan jumped.

"Sorry, love, I didn't mean to startle you." Kelly lightly scratched her back.

"It's okay. I just find it creepy here, that's all."

"I know. It's just bush, sand, and road but it's like we're surrounded by ghosts."

Rowan handed her the keys. "Your turn." She paused and looked at Kelly. "Know any good ghost stories?"

Just at that moment, they heard leaves rustling in the undergrowth and a crack as a tree snapped. A low moaning came to them on the foul wind.

"Fuck." Kelly dove into the car. "I don't want to know. I just want to get out of here."

She quickly pulled out of the rest stop.

Rowan looked in the side rear view mirror. The trees swayed and a shower of leaves pattered down into the rest stop. She saw a flash of something large and black as Kelly rounded the sweeper, blocking it from view. She shuddered.

"What?" Kelly asked.

"You don't want to know," Rowan said. "There was something coming to us from the undergrowth."

"What kind of something?"

"Big and black."

Kelly shuddered. "Oh, hell no. Not dealing with that."

"Yeah," Rowan said. "I wonder if that's why all the farmland looks so deserted? Weird things living in the bush?"

"I don't know," Kelly said. "I don't want to find out."

Rowan watched the clouds scudding across the sky. It was fully covered now in dark cloud, ominous and threatening.

Kelly rounded the last sweeper and they reached the small stretch of road that led by the abandoned Settler's Creek Motel. She pulled into the parking lot.

"You want to hole up here? Or go down to Ithaca?"

Rowan rolled down the window and took a deep breath of air. She smiled.

"What are you smiling about?" Kelly asked.

"The smell, Kell. It's gone." She turned to Kelly and grinned. "That horrible smell of rotting meat is gone. I think we're shifting realities. I don't think we need to worry about meteor showers or rain anymore."

Kelly wound down her own window and stuck her head out, breathing in the warmer air.

"We made it. We made it." She leant over and kissed Rowan. "This is awesome."

"Look at the motel," Rowan said.

They watched as the motel slowly came to life again. The building straightened and became whole again. The windows became clear and began to shine. The weeds in the asphalt slowly became transparent and winked out of existence as the asphalt darkened.

"I wonder if we have the same rooms?" Kelly said.

Rowan nodded. "I think so. Look." She nodded toward room three. The curtains drew closed and the *do not disturb* sign slowly swam into being on the doorknob of her room.

"This is fantastic," Rowan said. "You want to go down to Settler's Creek and get a bite to eat at that charming restaurant?"

"I admit it. I'm starved," Kelly said.

"Good. Let's go."

CHAPTER 21

"WHAT'S THAT COMING toward us?" Kelly asked, peering into the distance, in the direction of the stop sign.

Rowan stood shoulder to shoulder with her. "Oh, no. That looks like a bunch of armored vehicles." She looked straight at Kelly. "Get out of here."

"I don't want to do this. I don't want to leave you." Kelly looked into Rowan's eyes. "If we stay together, we have a better chance of shifting realities together. Remember what Glen said about Colonel Carne? What happens if they think that's me? It means I get free run of their facility and can get you out of there."

Rowan closed her eyes and sighed. "This time it's *me* that's screwed, not you." She looked straight at Kelly. "I need you to get me out of there. Go. Hide. Please."

Kelly felt sick. "I'm coming for you, Rowan. I promise you."

"I know. Go."

Kelly kissed her and ran toward her room. *I have no hope of getting into that room. I don't have my keys.* She veered toward reception and slipped inside as two jeeps rolled into the parking lot.

She hit the bell on the desk. The clerk came shuffling out a moment or so later. She tried to ignore the scuffle in the parking lot.

ROWAN STOOD IN the middle of the parking lot, trying to look relaxed. A man stood opposite her, a gun pointed at her head.

Oh, shit. This is not *good.*

"Can I help you?" she asked as he eyed her.

"You're under arrest, Doctor May. Come with me." He nodded to the soldiers in the jeeps. Two of them got out and before she knew what had happened, she was on the ground. The soldier yanked back her wrists and she grunted in pain.

He put handcuffs on her and they dragged her to her feet. *Oh shit. And who the hell is* Doctor May?

They put her into the back of the jeep with no particular gentleness.

The man with the gun got into the front seat and they silently left the parking lot, seemingly headed toward the Department of Defense.

Crap. I hope to God Kelly can get me, and soon. *I'm in serious shit.*

KELLY LEFT RECEPTION. There was no sign of Rowan. She felt like crying. Panic overtook her for a moment and she pushed it back.

Relax. Panicking's not going to help. I have to get into DoD. That's all. Focus, Kell. Okay. What can I use?

She went to her room and tried the door knob. It turned. It wasn't locked.

What the fuck?

She opened the door and stepped inside.

The shades were drawn and it was dark. She saw a familiar pile of luggage sitting in the small space between a built in wardrobe and dresser. She flicked on the lights and felt her skin crawl in shock. Her heart hammered.

A woman sat on the neatly made second bed. She was stock still and her cold eyes glittered with malice. She held a gun, pointed at Kelly.

Christ on a crutch. That's me. *Or my double, anyway. And oh, my God—she looks like a complete and utter* bitch.

"Do you mind if I sit down?" Kelly asked, gesturing toward the bed. She hoped the woman would say yes. Her knees were shaking.

The woman gave a short, sharp nod.

Kelly sat. They studied each other in silence.

They were the same height, but Kelly was more muscular. The woman also had a small scar over her right eyebrow. Kelly didn't have one of those. Kelly also thought Charles Manson had warmer eyes than the woman did.

"When I heard I'd been seen in Settler's Creek, I got curious," the woman said in a jarringly familiar voice.

Kelly remained silent.

"I thought that Adams was lying to me. Turns out he wasn't. He *was* from somewhere else."

The woman's use of past tense made Kelly's ears prick up. *Something's happened to Glen. I wonder if he's even still alive? I'm guessing not.*

"So I listened to the talk that went on around me. People were wondering why I was in the motel with a blonde. Doctor Rowan May. Of course it wasn't me. It had to be someone who looked like me. What better impersonator for me *than* me? Doctor May was right. We aren't cutting holes in outer space. We *are* crossing over into other realities. I knew finding my double was going to be easy. All I had to do was wait. Of course you came back." She smiled.

Kelly found her smile unpleasant.

"You *disgusting* pervert. People were saying how'd they'd seen us down at the restaurant together, engaged in the vilest of perversion. I asked how that could be. I *was* with Doctor May but we weren't there."

All we did was kiss in public. And where the hell is the real Doctor May?

"Where's Doctor May?" Kelly asked, trying to sound calm. Her hands were damp and shaking.

The woman gave her an unpleasant smile. "Next door. She's no one to trouble yourself with. She was diseased. There isn't a cure. It was such a pity. She was genetically *perfect*, yet unnatural and a pervert. God commands we put those types to death. What else is left for them but death anyway? They're certainly of no use to continue mankind."

This time Kelly had to fight down her gorge.

"Just imagine what everyone was thinking. About *me*." The woman shook her head in apparent revulsion. "The things they must have thought that the two of us were doing to each other. Kissing. Touching. Intimate contact. *Vile, unnatural* things." She took a shuddering breath. Her hand trembled.

Kelly shifted and the woman zeroed in on her again, cold eyes glittering with malice.

"*You.* This is *your* fault. What's *wrong* with you? It's *ungodly* to indulge your carnal lusts like that. Why did you choose *that* lifestyle? Am I so afraid of men in that other world? Could I not just find one? Don't you care about your *immortal soul?* Don't you want to be able to stand before the gates of heaven and proudly tell Saint Peter you've lived a godly life?"

Kelly wasn't religious. *Not particularly.* "At least I'm not going to have to tell him I murdered the woman I love."

The woman's eyes narrowed in rage and a look of revulsion swept over her features.

Bingo.

"I'm a god fearing woman, completely unlike *you*. I chose *not* to follow a life of perversion. I did *not* give into sin."

I'm guessing that she's really a lesbian. We have the same genetic patterns so we have the same sexual orientation. I'm able to live who I am openly and proudly, but she can't. Time to poke.

"I'll bet you wish you did, though. If *your* Rowan May was like *my* Rowan May, you'd know she's the one. She's your soul mate. She complements and completes you. She turns you on. You know you want to kiss your way up and down her body and not stop. You know you want to engage in the *vilest of perversions* all night long and you'd both love it."

The woman's eyes narrowed in rage. "I'm *not* like you."

"Oh, but I think you are. We're the *same* aren't we?"

"*We're nothing alike* at all," the woman screamed.

"Really? I'll bet you couldn't stop staring at her behind. I'll *bet* you wanted to suck on her breasts. I'll *bet* you wondered what she sounded like when she came." Kelly tilted her head, trying to look relaxed. She tensed up and prepared herself. "And I'll bet you'd have *loved* to find out what it felt like when she came in your mouth."

The woman was so red Kelly thought her head would explode.

"You evil whore," the woman screamed. "Blasphemer." She quickly stood and raised the gun, seemingly intent on battering Kelly to death instead of shooting her.

Kelly knew herself well. She stood at the same time as the woman and lunged forward. She lowered her head and head butted her as hard as she could. The woman was lighter than she was and flew backward and crashed head first into the dresser. She lay limp on the floor.

Kelly quickly knelt over her and felt for her pulse. There was none. Her temple had an ugly indent.

Oh fuck. I killed her. Fuck, fuck, fuck.

"I'm sorry. I didn't mean to do this to you." She settled back on her haunches. "I'm sure you were an ugly excuse for a human being. I'm sure you loved your Rowan and *wanted* to touch her. I'm not sure you knew it consciously. Then you killed the one thing that would have made your life redeeming. You *killed* Rowan. How's judgment day working out for you?"

She sighed. "I'm sorry. I love my Rowan and admit it. I need your access card to go and get her."

The woman was dressed like a fifties housewife. She wore a skirt, blouse, and high heels. Kelly wondered if she normally wore a uniform or if she always dressed like that. She felt her for pockets. There were none.

She was waving a gun at me. She's not wearing a holster. I wonder if she's deviant *enough to be carrying a handbag?*

Kelly did a quick inventory of the bags on the floor. They were all hers. She sighed in frustration. She glanced up at the bed and a black shape caught her eye. She felt strong distaste as she picked up the woman's purse and began rifling through it. Make up, keys, and wallet. Nothing else. No official ID, swipe card or anything that might have gotten her into the Department of Defense.

Kelly stuffed the keys into her pocket and took out the wallet. She rifled through it. She pulled out the woman's driver's license and smiled. *I've got her address. Now we're in business.*

She jogged from the room and paused. *Do I really want to know?*

She went to Rowan's room and tried the door knob. It wasn't locked. She pushed open the door and braced herself.

Oh, Jesus Christ. Oh, God. A badly injured version of Rowan was lying on the bed and Kelly had to force herself to go to her. Her knees were shaking and she felt sick. *They had sex and the other me killed her.*

The bare woman on the bed had been shot. Blood lay in a thick pool beneath her on twisted sheets, soaking into the mattress. She moaned softly.

Oh shit. She's still alive. Kelly knelt by the side of the bed. Her face felt wet and she brushed away tears.

She smoothed the woman's damp hair back from her sweaty forehead. She looked so much like her Rowan that Kelly felt herself split open.

The woman's eyes fluttered open and widened in terror as she saw Kelly.

"Easy," Kelly said softly. "I'm not Colonel Carne. I'm Kelly Carne but I'm not from this place."

The woman on the bed sighed and nodded.

"I don't have much time left," the woman said slowly, gasping for breath. "You have to leave. Our reality is destabilizing."

Kelly nodded. "I'm going to get my Rowan and we're going home."

"Soon. This world won't exist for much longer."

"As soon as I can get into DoD, we're leaving."

The woman nodded and closed her eyes.

Kelly leant over and gently kissed her forehead. "I know this won't make up for what's happened to you. I know I can't make it right, or help you, or be yours in this reality. *Your* Kelly Carne is gone. *My* Rowan is here. I love her with all my heart and soul. She's the love of my life and I'd do anything for her. I think we're the same in all worlds."

The woman on the bed gave her the ghost of a smile. She took a final, deep breath and exhaled.

Kelly put a gentle hand on the woman's chest. She was gone. Kelly let out her own deep breath. *What a waste.*

She stood, feeling sad, wanting her Rowan more than ever.
I have to get moving if I'm going to get my *Rowan.*
She left, closing the door gently behind her.

Rowan sat waiting in a room just inside the doors of where the administration offices were in her reality. The soldiers had brought her in there and left her.

SHE GLANCED AROUND. Four white walls, metal table, and chairs. Otherwise bare. There were no windows and nowhere to look, so she traced patterns on the table top, trying to calm her jangling nerves.

I hope Kelly's all right. I hope she comes and gets me soon. This feels bad.

She heard the door knob and forced herself not to look. The door opened, footsteps entered the room, and came to a halt beside her.

"It's about time you got here," she said, without looking up.

"We were wondering where you were," a man's said voice. "Jenson said you left with Colonel Carne."

Rowan looked up at him, keeping her expression carefully neutral.

He was tall, a few inches over her six feet. He had blonde hair and blue eyes. His eyes were ice cold. *He looks like a stereotype Nazi. Fatigues don't suit him at all.*

He indicated the chair opposite her. "Do you mind if I sit down?"

As if I had a choice. Rowan nodded. "Be my guest."

He sat down and stared at her. She felt like she wanted to fidget and forced herself to remain still.

"I suppose you want to know why you're here, Doctor May."

Doctor *May? Who* am *I here?* Rowan remained silent.

"You were seen leaving with Colonel Carne."

"Is that a crime?"

"It is if you're a pervert."

Oh, shit. The restaurant. Rowan tilted her head at him. "Explain."

"You have . . . *unnatural* . . . inclinations, don't you?"

"In what sense?"

"You're having relations with her, aren't you?"

"No, I'm not." *Well, not Colonel Carne, at least.*

"Are you sure?"

"I think I'd remember something like that."

"You were seen together a few nights ago at a restaurant in Settler's Creek."

"Eating? Yes. I do that every now and again."

"You were indulging unnatural lusts."

Gnocchi Neopolitana is hardly unnatural. "I have done *nothing* like that with Colonel Carne."

He stared at her.

She stared back.

The moment was broken by the soft knock at the door.

"Enter," the man said.

A soldier opened the door. "Sir? Sorry to disturb you, Sir. Doctor Irwin requests your presence in the lab right away."

There was something in his tone that made Rowan eye him carefully. The soldier looked pale and a little frightened.

The blue-eyed man nodded. "I will go now." He nodded toward Rowan. "Keep an eye on her. Don't let her leave."

Rowan sighed inwardly as they both left the room. The lock clicked a moment later.

Kelly. I need you, Kelly.

CHAPTER 22

KELLY CAUTIOUSLY MADE her way down the winding road toward Settler's Creek. It was slow going. There were military trucks on the road, more than she remembered from when they'd gone down into the town for dinner. *At least Rowan's car fits in nicely here. Where does the other me live?* She glanced at the driver's license in her hand. *Calvert Creek Road.*

The road began to flatten out as she reached the bottom of the hill. *Why does Calvert Creek Road ring bells?* She pulled up at the stop sign. The left led to the restaurant they'd had dinner at. Right looked like it led nowhere and straight ahead went into the town of Settler's Creek. *Town is the most likely place for her to live.*

She went straight ahead through the stop sign. More army trucks passed her. *Why are all the army guys out?*

She drove into the small town. It seemed mostly deserted; there weren't any cars on the road and the stores were all closed and darkened. It was full night. She passed a bus stop and quickly hit the brakes. *Was that a map on the wall of the bus stop?* She looked over her shoulder and saw that she was alone on the road. She put the car into reverse and quickly backed up to the bus stop. *God I hope there are no cops around. I have to get to Rowan.*

She quickly got out and jogged up to the sign indicating what the bus stop was. There was a bus route and a schedule bolted to the pole. She leant forward, trying to read the dusty and weathered sign.

That's interesting. And good. I'm on *Calvert Creek Road.* She looked down at the license she still held in her hand. *Unit One, twenty one. Okay.* She looked around. *Frustrating. These buildings don't have numbers on them.* She jogged back to the car and got in.

She heard a concussion in the distance and saw a flash of light in the rear view mirror. *What the hell?* A bright light, like a searchlight, shone up into the night sky. She followed the beam up and saw the stars and immediately looked away, heart beating hard. *Oh, fuck. What the hell is that?* She looked upward again. She'd been right. The stars did look like they were quivering uneasily in the sky. The ground moved beneath the car and she glanced around at building numbers. *It's starting. I have to get to Rowan.*

She drove past what looked like a combination convenience and clothing store. There was a large number nineteen over the door. She stopped before the next building and peered at it. *Yep. That's twenty one.*

She got out of the car and put the keys in her pocket. She locked the doors and jogged to the front door of the building. *Why is it so light out now? I thought it was after sunset?* She looked around. There was definitely more light, a ghostly and flickering orange. It was almost like fire. *Get in and get out. That's all I have to do.*

Her hands were shaking and it took a couple of tries to unlock the door. She slipped inside. The hallway had an air of desolation that almost suggested the entire building was empty except for Colonel Kelly Carne. She glanced over at the mail boxes.

Figures. All of the labels are blank except for two of them. Doctor May and Colonel Carne lived in the same building.

She took another step forward and the foyer was flooded with light. *Sensors. Nice.*

There was a door just up ahead of her to the left. It was unit one. She tried the keys one by one until one slid into the lock. She turned it and the door opened with a satisfying click.

She felt for a light switch and flicked it. The room was flooded with light.

This is much neater than my place but it's so devoid of personality it might as well be a display home. The living room had a lounge and two recliners in it. The walls were bare except for a reproduction of The Last Supper and a crucifix with a smaller, palm crucifix tucked in behind the brass Jesus. A worn bible lay haphazardly on the coffee table, the only sign of disorder. To the left was a kitchen. It looked stringent and neat, with marble countertops and expensive-looking appliances. There was a hallway just ahead of her that went down to the left. She went to it, turning on lights as she went.

She stuck her head into a bathroom, so neat and clean that it looked like she could eat off the floors. Further down were three doors. One led to an immaculate linen closet, the second was the master bedroom and the final one was locked.

I'll bet I can guess what she was hiding. Kelly rifled through the keys and picked a small brass one. She tried it and the door unlocked. She pushed it open and went inside. She blinked. It was a spare bedroom. The bed looked soft and comfortable. There was a television set and bedside tables. There were also piles of stacked magazines and DVDs under the television stand.

She inspected the stack of magazines. She picked up the top two. *Lipstick Lezzies? And Dirty Dykes? Fuck me, pardon the pun.* She opened the magazine. It was stuffed full of pictures of naked women and graphic sex. The next magazine on the pile was *Playboy.* She pulled out more of the magazines and almost all of it was hardcore lesbian porn.

She bent over and looked at the DVDs. *Lick It Up? Fucking Housewives? Executives Who Like It Hard? Girls On Girls? Holy shit. I'm sure she's got some collector's editions in here. I'm not going to look under the bed. I'm sure she's got a seventy-two piece set of metric dildos.* No wonder *she keeps this room locked. She was probably terrified of thieves.* She snorted. *It'd be the ultimate in hypocrisy for a bloody redneck. And I'm guessing she tells everyone she keeps this stuff so she can keep up with the perverts and their current crop of filth.* She stood. She felt sick. *I have to stop gaping like an idiot. I have to get moving. This isn't helping. All it does is confirm what I already know.*

She left the room, locking it behind her. *Why bother? No one's ever going to be in here again.*

She went into the master bedroom. *Where do I normally*

keep my work stuff? Bedside table drawers, maybe? She rifled through the bedside table drawers and came up empty. She went on to the dresser drawers and found nothing besides an impressive collection of skimpy lingerie.

She sighed. *Where the hell would I put that stuff?* She thought a moment. *If she's like me she's prone to forgetting her key card. So if I have to remember it, I put it right by the front door where I can't avoid seeing it. I'm going to take a quick look in the kitchen.*

She made her way back up the hallway, flinching as she went past the spare room. She turned out the lights behind her. She went back into the doorway to the living room and carefully scanned the walls. *Ah. Got it.* She went to a small sequence of hooks hung by the front door and pulled up a badge. She stared at the picture. Colonel Carne stared grimly out of the picture as though the photographer had been engaged in crimes against humanity when the picture was taken. There was also a set of keys and Kelly took those as well. She left the unit, flicking off the last of the lights with a sigh. She looked down the hallway toward Rowan's unit. She wanted to go to it so badly she twitched.

No. Focus. You want your *Rowan, not the one you couldn't help.*

She jogged out of the block of units and stopped dead.

There was an army jeep parked beside Rowan's car, making it impossible for her to drive away.

"Colonel Carne," one man said, an officer by his bearing. "We've been looking for you. Can you come with us, please?"

Kelly's heart rate picked up and she went cold.

ROWAN DIDN'T KNOW how long she was stuck in the small interrogation room for. She was hungry and thirsty.

She looked around, wondering if it was a good idea to yell to anyone who would listen that she was still there.

She stared at the walls for a little longer, her palms damp with sweat. *I can't wait anymore. I want out of here.*

She stood and began to pace.

She just reached the door and jumped back as it unlocked and opened.

A balding man wearing a lab coat stuck his head in the door. "Rowan?"

Rowan gave a single nod. She wondered who he was. She saw an embossed *Brannigan* on his lab coat.

"Come with me. We have a problem."

She took a step toward him. "What's up?"

He looked at her carefully, raking her with his gaze from top to bottom.

"Rick," he said so softly she almost missed it.

"Rick. Talk to me," she said a little more loudly.

"We have a problem. We're getting power spikes."

"Show me."

Rick held the door open and gestured for her to go ahead of him. The two armed guards exchanged a glance and one wearing corporal's stripes put a hand on Rick's arm.

Rick stopped, looked at the soldier, and then gave him a pointed look.

"I'm sorry, Doctor Brannigan. Doctor May isn't allowed out of this room."

"By whose authority?" Rick asked.

"Major Styles."

"Send Major Styles my way when he gets back. Tell him we have a code red, do you understand me? A *code red*."

Rick dragged Rowan away before the soldiers could react.

"You know I'm not from here, don't you?" Rowan whispered when they were out of earshot.

Rick shook his head slightly and remained silent. He led her over to the lift. He punched the button and after a couple of seconds the lift doors opened. They silently went down to the basement. He led her past the darkened computer room to a set of lifts at the rear of the building.

This lift was utilitarian and utterly bare of any comforts, including light. Rowan could see concrete walls through the wire cage that surrounded them. There was light below them and after a second or so they descended into a vast concrete chamber. It was almost deserted and the lift shook. Rowan shot Rick a questioning glance.

"Earthquake," he said. "Follow me."

The lift slid to a stop and Rick unfastened a gate that Rowan hadn't noticed. They got out of the lift. The chamber was deserted.

Rowan had to shout to make herself heard over the throbbing of giant machinery. "Where is everyone?"

"Everyone's been evacuated. No point, really, but it's safety regulations."

"Why are we getting earthquakes? Australia's not prone to earthquakes."

"It is now," Rick said as he gestured toward a large steel room to one side.

There was a flash of light and for a second Rowan thought she saw rocks around her.

"I know," Rick said.

She glanced at him.

"I saw it too." He swiped his card across the reader outside the control room and they went inside.

The sudden silence felt deafening to Rowan.

"They have cameras down here but I disabled the mikes. We can talk."

"You said you knew I wasn't from here."

"And you're not. You're from another reality, aren't you?"

"Yes. I'm not from here." *Why lie? Something's horribly wrong.*

The earth shook again and Rick grabbed a chair to keep from falling over.

There was a blinding flash of white light. Ghosts of soldiers and people in lab coats winked in and out of existence.

"You shouldn't have come here," Rick said. "This world is about to end. We don't have much more than maybe an hour or two."

Rowan felt her blood run cold. *Kelly.*

CHAPTER 23

KELLY GOT INTO the jeep and a soldier slid in on either side of her, sandwiching her into position.

"You want to tell me what's going on?" she asked. She looked around, frowning. It was supposed to be full night but she could easily make out the features of the men sitting around her.

The jeep started off back down Calvert Creek Road.

"You're needed in the control room," the soldier said. "That's all I know. Orders are from Major Styles."

Kelly nodded as though she understood what he was talking about. She looked up at the ridge as they rounded a sweeper. The entire ridge was bathed in ghostly orange flames that gave off incandescent light. The trees they burned looked untouched.

A search light from the fire pit in the middle of the fire shone up into the heavens above.

"The flames aren't real, ma'am," a private said softly. He stared straight ahead of him.

"I gathered, soldier," Kelly said dryly. "I can't feel any heat."

"Quiet, private," the corporal said.

They drove through the stop sign without slowing and began the ascent up the hill to the Department of Defense. They found themselves behind a convoy. The driver flashed his lights and honked the horn. The trucks in the convoy pulled over and allowed them to pass. The jeep accelerated up the hill through a burst of white light. Kelly thought she saw ghostly horses and cars. A dull rumbling began in the distance, immense and all consuming. The ground shook a second or so later.

The sky overhead brightened as the sun came up.

Kelly looked up, alarmed. She tried to remain expressionless. Watching the sun scud across the sky terrified her. She looked straight ahead and steeled herself. They reached the top of the ridge and the ground moved in a slow, stomach-turning wave. Ghostly fire raced around them.

Kelly saw someone moving in the fire. He was as ghostly as the twenty foot flames were. He himself was on fire and he thrashed and soundlessly screamed as he careened off the burning trees.

Dear God. Kelly fought down her gorge. He finally collapsed in the flames, lighting up more of the bush around him. The soldiers ignored him as they drove past his burning carcass. *He looks like barbecue. I hope to God he's dead.*

They drove through the boom gates and up to the main doors of the Department of Defense.

A cold, blonde-haired and blue-eyed man approached them. He eyed her suspiciously.

I hope this is Major Styles. "Major?"

The blonde man saluted. "Colonel." He gestured toward the doors. "I was just on my way down to see Doctor Brannigan."

"Do you know what he wants?" Kelly asked, striding toward the lift with the Major by her side. *At least I'm in the same building with Rowan.*

"No, ma'am." He eyed her. "May I speak freely, ma'am?"

"No. *I* will go down to see Doctor Brannigan," Kelly said as the lift doors opened. She gestured toward the corporal who had met her at Colonel Carne's block of flats. "Keep him here. Don't let him leave." She turned back toward the major. "Don't *try* to leave. If you do, I'll have you shot."

She stepped into the lift and hit the button for the basement. The doors closed before the major could protest, and long enough for her to see the corporal take a step toward him.

Good. Rid of him. I have to try and find Rowan. This isn't the perfect place to start. She won't be down here. Doesn't matter. I have to look here anyway. At least this way I can *check the basement.*

The lift slowed to a stop and the doors opened. She found herself outside the eerily familiar basement computer room.

A light against the far wall, distorted through the glass, caught her eye. *Hah. There* is *a lift at the back of the computer room.*

She went down to it and hit the car call button. The lift rumbled to a stop and the doors opened seconds later. *Wow. That lift is bare, isn't it?*

She got in the lift and hit the only button in there. It was labeled *Generator.* The lift began to rumble down. Suddenly there was a flash of bright light, almost blinding her. She blinked, trying to decide if there were rocks directly in front of her face or not.

The elevator slid to a halt in a massive, concrete cavern. She opened the gate and stepped out of the lift, looking all around in amazement. *Dear God, this place is big enough to have its own weather. And it's almost completely empty.* She saw an enclosed structure to one side and headed toward it.

There was massive machinery in the middle of the room and it seemed to generate its own light from within. The light pulsed queasily at odd intervals. She could almost hear a sub aural humming. It set her teeth on edge. The machinery filled her with terror and she steeled herself, trying to ignore it. Panic wouldn't help her find Rowan. *Not that leaving is going to work for us anyway. Shit.*

The door to the structure swung open and a man in a lab coat came out. He was holding a gun, pointed at her.

"Hey. Take it easy." She put up her hands. "I'm not going to hurt you. I'm looking for someone."

The man, much closer now, eyed her suspiciously and then slowly lowered the gun.

The door to the structure flew open and Rowan came jogging out.

"Rowan," Kelly called. "Are you all right? No one hurt you?"

Rowan engulfed her in a smothering hug and kissed her. Kelly returned the kiss, loving the feel of Rowan's strong body in her arms.

"I'm fine." Rowan smoothed Kelly's hair away from her forehead. "You, love?"

"I'm good. We have to get out of here. The world is destabilizing."

Rowan glanced at the lab coated man. "We know. This is Rick."

The man, Rick, stared at her. "You look so much like Colonel Carne. It's incredible."

"I'm not Colonel Carne." Kelly felt her face heat. "Colonel Carne won't be coming back here."

Rick nodded. "Have you seen Doctor May?"

"She's dead."

"Oh, no." He shook his head. "Leaving here won't help you. The entire world is going to implode in at most an hour. What happened to Rowan?" He glanced at Rowan. "Um, Doctor May?"

"Colonel Carne shot her."

"Why on earth did she do that?"

Kelly glanced at Rowan, who looked pale. *Do I tell him Colonel Carne shot her after they slept together?* She glanced up at the wall. A crucifix hung on it. *Interesting. Glen was right. They* are *all Jesus freaks here.*

"I think she and Colonel Carne slept together. The colonel couldn't deal with it and killed her."

Rick went pale. He collapsed in a nearby chair. "So that was why she wasn't selected for the lifeboat. That's why she was ejected from the eugenics program. That's why they never selected her for the breeding program."

Kelly gaped at him. *Eugenics? Breeding?*

"I can see everyone here is a homophobe," Rowan said. "Got it. But a *eugenics* program? What the hell is going on here? Why did you build this generator thing?"

"We built it to preserve the sanctity of our race," Rick said. "At least that's what the Protection For Families party told everyone. God spoke to them and told them to build an ark since end of times were on us. A holocaust would sweep over us because the almighty had been defied too many times by unbelievers, idolaters, and so on."

Rowan rolled her eyes. "So they built one and everyone marched onto it two by two."

"Only the most Godly of us were selected to go onto the ark. We were surprised Rowan wasn't called for anything. She's intelligent, a wonderful specimen of physical perfection and her offspring would have been dominant if bred with the right stock."

Rowan's eyebrows drew together. Her shoulders tensed.

The world filled with a brilliant flash of pure, white light. Kelly held up her hand. It was almost as though she could see the bones through her skin.

Ghostly people flickered uneasily into being. One of them was Rowan in a lab coat, next to an equally ghostly Rick Brannigan. The ghostly Rowan's eyes widened at the sight of her and she nudged the ghostly Rick. They both winked out of existence.

Rick sat on a chair behind a panel clutching his head.

"What happened to the Ark?" Kelly asked, nudging Rick's shoulder.

"We sent it through a worm hole. We thought we were sending it to another planet, but we were really sending it to another reality. I think we actually saw you." His voice trailed off. He looked up at them again, his expression earnest and beseeching. "I'm sorry. I don't know what's going to happen now, besides the destabilization of our reality. This world will cease to exist. I wish we could go back and stop this experiment from ever happening."

"Do you even know how your reality came about?" Rowan asked.

Rick shook his head.

The ground shook beneath their feet and Kelly clutched at Rowan. "I'm scared."

Rowan's bright blue eyes were calm and confident. She gazed into Kelly's eyes. "Relax, love. No matter what happens, we're together. At least we're both still alive."

The ground shook again and this time they were both knocked over. Kelly landed on Rowan. A dull rumbling started up. It was gigantic and unstoppable. Kelly clutched at Rowan, burying her face into Rowan's neck. Rowan's arms tightened around her.

There was another gigantic flash of light.

ROWAN FELT AS though she'd been knocked over onto her back. She looked down and realized that it felt that way because it was true. She *was* on her back and Kelly was on top of her. Kelly shifted and Rowan watched as two of her peeled away.

She looked around. They were up at the fire pit. A filthy man dressed in pants, a shirt, and worn boots sat by the fire. He had a billy resting in the flames and he pushed the logs. A shower of sparks leapt up into the sky.

He stood and stretched.

There was a bright flash of white light.

Rowan blinked. The swag man looked around uncertainly.

A ghostly figure swam into being. It was a man in a silver suit. The hobo stared at him. He took an uncertain step backward. The silver-suited man stepped toward him.

He took a step forward as the ground trembled. He stumbled and fell into the fire pit. He became a human torch and screamed soundlessly at them. He stumbled forward, waving his arms, trying to put out the fire.

The silver man kicked at him and two ghostly fire men peeled away from him. One fell down the slope toward Ithaca and the other fell to the other side, toward Settler's Creek. The silver suited man winked out of existence.

The ground heaved and there was another flash of bright light.

This time Rowan saw the entire ridge as a ball of orange flame. The ground split open. At the same time, a jet of pure, white light shot toward the sky and it almost looked like the moon tore itself apart.

A loud rumbling, louder than Rowan had ever heard before, filled the air. The ground split open under them and they fell. She automatically grabbed for Kelly, pulling her in close as they plummeted downward through burning air.

Kelly's arms tightened around her and she buried her face into Rowan's chest.

There was a gigantic bolt of white light, the brightest yet, and Rowan knew no more.

CHAPTER 24

ROWAN'S EYES FLUTTERED open and for one, terrible moment, she didn't know where she was. Then she realized she was lying flat on her back in her bed. It was her own bedroom ceiling that she was looking at. She stretched an arm out beside her, half expecting to feel a warm body there with her, but the sheets were cool. She was alone. She felt a terrible, heavy longing. She glanced at the bedside table, at her clock. It showed five thirty in the morning.

No, I'm wide awake. I won't be going back to sleep any time soon. What a horrible dream. Something about Kelly Carne, meteors, rain, and bright light. The dream slipped away from her the more she tried to hold onto it, but the terrible sensation of rushing headlong into disaster remained. She grabbed her watch from the nightstand. She blinked. It was Saturday.

What the hell happened all week? What did I do yesterday? Wait. What did I do all week? She looked at the bare sheets beside her. *Why do I feel like I'm missing someone?* It was silly. She felt like she'd broken up with someone, it wasn't mutual, and she'd been on the receiving end of the bad news. A heavy feeling of longing settled over her.

Oh, for Christ's sake. I'm unattached. I've been that way for a few years. Maybe I need to get laid. She thought about finding a willing woman but immediately shied away from the prospect. *Nope. Don't want to do that.*

She sat up and swung her legs over the side of the bed. "Maybe a run would do me some good?" She stood with a heavy-hearted sigh and looked for her running shorts and a tee shirt.

An image of Kelly Carne's beautiful face flashed through her mind and left her feeling more dejected than before. *God, what is the* matter *with me? She's a co-worker.* A small voice at the back of her mind spoke up. *Yes, but you want so much more out of her, don't you?* She sighed. *I want her. I admit it. But I can't have her. I accept that.* The voice spoke again. *Call her. Talk to her. Take her out for coffee today or tomorrow and make your move. You've waited long enough, and this whole school girl mooning over a classmate thing is* old. *Get over it and make her yours.*

Rowan wondered who the small voice actually belonged to. She pulled on her running clothes and shoes and strapped on her watch. It was a quarter to six. *Too early to call her but I'll send her a quick text.* She took her cell phone off the bedside table and quickly tapped out a message before she could lose confidence. She dimly realized that her hands were shaking. *Happy now? I'm going to go for a run. You can make me check my messages when I get back.*

She tossed her phone on the bed and left.

KELLY WOKE UP at the soft sound of her cell phone beeping, telling her that she had a message. She felt an incredible sadness as the vestiges of a bad dream slowly drew deep inside her again. Her heart felt heavy with heartache.

She heard a soft groan from beside her and Genevieve's dark eyes opened.

"God, not again," Genevieve said. "You should just tell them to get fucked. It's the weekend—*Saturday morning*—for Christ's sake."

Kelly felt a slow wave of dislike wash over her, leaving her feeling irritated and wanting to leave. *What a gigantic nag. I'm over this. I'm going to end it. I've had enough. That being said, leaving's not easy when you share the same house.* She picked up her cell phone and got out of bed. She padded naked to the kitchen, hitting buttons as she went. She flicked on the coffee maker.

She stopped dead. *What's Rowan want at this time of morning?* A bolt of happy anticipation shot through her. She opened the message and read it.

Hey, Kell. I know it's the weekend, it's early, you're probably busy and you're attached, but do you want to go to lunch with me or something? I just want to talk.

Well, well, well. Kelly looked back in the direction of the bedroom. She felt a strong shot of dislike. She thought about Rowan and felt happy. She also felt a surge of attraction and allowed it to go through her.

Sure, she typed. *You're going to have to come and pick me up, though. About twelve?* She typed out her address and hit send.

That's phase one of Operation Freedom. Now comes phase two.

She padded back into the bedroom and sat on the edge of the bed. Genevieve rolled over and opened her eyes.

"What do they want *this* time, Kelly? You give them everything for free. If you have to work, how about this time you make them *pay* you for it."

"I wasn't asked to go to work today. And if I was, I don't need—or want—your permission to do it. In fact, it's none of your business. Neither is my salary, my time off, or my life."

Genevieve's eyes widened, and she sat up. The sheets pooled around her waist. "Why are you being like this, Kell? I thought we were a team. I love you."

Kelly steeled herself. "I don't believe you. And I don't love you, Genevieve. I haven't for a while. I don't want to be with you anymore."

"Can we work through this?"

"No. We're done. I'm not stupid. You don't care about me, you care about my paycheck. I've *never* appeared at the top of your priority list, so I'm not sure why you think you should be at the top of mine. I'm not part of your life but you expect to be part of mine. I'm done. Not only do I not love you, I don't particularly like you." Kelly stood. "Get your stuff and get out."

Genevieve gave her a cold look. "I don't know why you're being such a bitch. I've never understood why you do it. You're dull, self-centered and unambitious."

Kelly bit down her temper. "And you need to leave."

"Actually," Genevieve said as she got out of bed. "I don't need to do anything of the sort. Our names are *both* on the lease. If you want to call it off, go find yourself somewhere else to live."

"More than happy to do it, Gen," Kelly said with a sigh. *I'm not going to argue with her and I don't like this place. She chose it for us without my input.* She felt a dull spurt of anger and forced it down. "However, since *my* name is *also* on the lease, I don't have to go anywhere. I'm going to move into the spare room."

"It's full of boxes. You're going to sleep on the floor?"

"No. I'm going to sleep on the couch buried under all that shit. And *you* are going to clean out that room. It's full of *your* shit. Not mine. You already threw out everything I had before we moved in together. Unless you want me to return the compliment, I suggest you get your fucking crap out of my living area."

Kelly left. Rage was flooding through her system and she wasn't sure she could control herself enough not to tear off Genevieve's arms and beat her to death with them.

She grabbed her robe as went. She went into the kitchen and poured herself a cup of freshly brewed coffee. She looked at her phone. There was a message from Rowan.

Cool, I'll see you at around twelve, then.

The sense of happiness increased and the dull feeling of pain lifted. *Do I want to wait until the middle of the day?*

She began typing. *I just broke up with my girlfriend. I want out of the house. Are you up for breakfast?* She hit send.

She went back into the bedroom and began picking up clothes to wear for the day. Genevieve gave her a quick, guilty look as she entered the bedroom. Her cell phone was in her hand and her other hand was half cupped over the speaker.

Kelly rolled her eyes. "For Christ's sake, I know you're cheating on me. Be honest about it. I don't care. Just talk openly to your little piece on the side."

Genevieve gave her a look loaded with dislike. Kelly's phone beeped softly. She looked down at it.

I'll be there in an hour, was Rowan's message. Kelly smiled happily.

She padded into the bathroom, feeling as though a weight had lifted from her shoulders.

ROWAN FELT LIKE wagging her tail. Kelly was unattached. She'd finally broken up with her girlfriend.

I never met her but I hated her.

She stripped off her sweaty jogging gear and went into the bathroom. She had a leisurely shower and checked her watch. She still had half an hour before she had to meet Kelly.

I don't want to wait. I want to go now.

She scooped her keys up off the counter and went out to her company car. She got in and backed out of the driveway. *It's a beautiful, sunny day and I get to indulge myself with Kelly. This is so cool.*

The traffic was light and finding Kelly's flat was easy. She slowly drove up the alleyway behind the units, as Kelly had told her to do. She was just starting a text message to her to let her know she was waiting when she saw Kelly's elegant figure appear out of the back gate.

She got out of the car and Kelly's face creased into a broad grin. Before she knew what was happening, Kelly was running toward her and launched herself at her. Rowan caught her easily, swung her around, and held on tight.

Kelly shifted in her arms and looked deep into her eyes. Rowan felt as though she was possessed. She leant up and kissed Kelly, long and deep, tasting her. Kelly returned her kiss, tasting her in turn.

Rowan rested her forehead against Kelly's when they broke. "Good morning to you too, Kell."

"I'm sorry," Kelly said breathlessly. "I know I shouldn't have done that but I've always *wanted* to do it."

A deep sense of peace and contentment settled over Rowan. She smiled and kissed Kelly again. "So have I, truth be told." She took a deep, uneven breath. "Why now, Kell? Why?"

"I'm tired of living with someone who doesn't love me. I'm tired of being right in front of you, wishing we were together, wanting you, and not having you. I want there to be an *us*. Life is too short to be miserable."

Rowan felt déjà vu. She felt as though they'd had something and it'd gone for some reason. *It feels like we're trying again.*

Kelly read her expression perfectly. "If there was an *us*, we didn't break up because we weren't good together. It was something else."

Rowan felt almost drunk with happiness. "I'm all for taking up where we never left off."

Kelly laughed, and then abruptly sobered. "I had a dream last night. You were part of it, I think. I need to talk to you about it."

Rowan nodded. She thought about the flashes of memory she'd had when she'd woken up. "I'm happy to listen. I feel the same thing." She smoothed Kelly's hair away from her forehead. "Where do you want to go for breakfast?"

"Somewhere quiet."

"We could go back to my place? It's quiet. No ex-girlfriends, no crowds. Just peace and quiet."

"I'm game."

Rowan took her hand and led her to the car. She opened the door with a flourish and Kelly climbed in. She got in and started the engine. She completed a quick turn and glanced in her mirror.

"Is that your ex?" she said, nodding at the reflection of the woman in the rear view mirror.

Kelly looked over her shoulder. She groaned. "Yes."

"I know it's not nice to speak badly of other people, but I have to say it. I don't like your ex. I never did. I always thought she was cruel to you."

Kelly nodded. "I agree. I'm glad it's done."

Rowan watched as Kelly's ex stood in the middle of the road and made an obscene gesture at the car. She dialed a number on her cell phone and strode back toward the flat.

Kelly settled her hand on Rowan's thigh and squeezed gently.

A wave of desire broke over Rowan. She gently trapped Kelly's hand, lifted it, and kissed Kelly's knuckles.

They were back at Rowan's house fifteen minutes later. Rowan opened the front door with a flourish. *Should I pick her up and carry her over the threshold? I want to.*

"Are you going to go in?" Kelly frowned slightly, her gaze turned inward.

Déjà vu washed over Rowan. *This time I'm going to do things differently.*

She smiled at Kelly and easily scooped her up. She carried Kelly in. Kelly blushed and laughed. She put her arms around Rowan's neck. Rowan gently set her back on her feet.

"What was that for?" Kelly asked.

"Because I wanted to." Rowan gazed at Kelly, trying to force back images of slipping Kelly's blouse off her shoulders and nibbling on her breasts.

Kelly's gaze turned predatory and she advanced on Rowan. She tore off Rowan's shirt and began nipping her breasts.

Rowan's mind scattered and she moaned, holding Kelly's face against her bare breasts. Kelly paused in her assault and took Rowan by the hand, almost dragging her to the bedroom. They barely made it to the bed.

Kelly lay in Rowan's arms afterward, snuggled against her. She looked content.

"How did you know where my bedroom was?" Rowan asked. "Not that I mind, of course. But you've never been here before."

"I feel like I have," Kelly said. "I'm glad you don't have nudes on the walls."

Rowan's eyebrows shot skyward. "Pardon me?"

"This house looks familiar. I feel like I know the layout. The décor is different to what I was half expecting." She took a deep breath. "I know we got distracted." Kelly rolled over and looked into Rowan's eyes. "We really *do* have to talk. It feels like I know this place well."

Rowan stole a kiss. "Let me make you some breakfast."

Kelly nodded. "Yeah. I really *do* need to talk." Her gaze lingered on Rowan's breasts. "And you're *very* distracting."

Rowan grinned. She felt almost drunk with happiness, but the lingering feeling of disaster from her dream filtered through her. She slowly sat up, her eyes glued to Kelly's face.

"Let's see how well you know my house."

Kelly nodded, her dark eyes intent. They got out of bed, and Kelly grabbed two robes from inside Rowan's wardrobe. They slipped them on.

Kelly took her by the hand, and they went into the kitchen.

"What would you like for breakfast?" Rowan asked softly.

"Scrambled eggs and toast." Kelly pulled out a skillet and they began making breakfast.

After they'd finished eating, they stacked the dishwasher and sat next to each other on the sofa, sipping cups of coffee.

"Okay," Rowan said with a sigh. "Do you want to start or shall I?"

"You first," Kelly said, snuggling into her.

CHAPTER 25

"I HAD A dream last night," Rowan said. "It was a bad one, I know that. You were in it. I'm guessing we were lovers."

Kelly grinned, watching Rowan's face darken as she blushed. "It's okay, love. Just tell me."

"We were in a motel in the middle of nowhere. It was a wreck. We kept going past what looked like an office building to a fire pit at the end of the road. We were trying to make our way back to Sydney, my house, the office. Whatever. I remember that the world looked like it was dying. The sky was a really ugly shade of purplish green. The rain was yellowish. We got caught in a meteor storm."

Kelly felt a wave of unreality wash over her. "Do you remember anything about homophobes, and that it was really cold out? Soldiers?"

Rowan's brilliant blue eyes blazed with intensity. "A computer room that was really creepy? A gigantic underground cavern?"

Kelly nodded. She felt slightly nauseated.

"And," Rowan continued, "it all started with a site visit, right?"

Kelly's mind worked at the speed of light. *What site visits have we gone to lately that involve a trip to the countryside?* She nodded. "Give me a moment, I'm trying to remember."

"Another thing. Do you know what the day and date are today?"

"Today is Saturday, March seventh."

Rowan nodded. "True. But when I woke up this morning, it felt like March fourteen." She smiled. "Now it just feels like Christmas."

Kelly grinned at that. "To answer your first question, we haven't had any site visits of over a day in the past month or so. We do, however, have something coming up on Monday. Glen flies out tomorrow. It's Department of Defense, up in Settler's

Creek. In Queensland." She almost flinched as she said it and wondered why.

Rowan looked puzzled for a moment. "Tell him to check in. Often. Like, at lunch and at the end of the day."

"He's going to think I'm nuts. But I agree."

They were quiet for a moment as they sipped their coffee. Kelly snuggled into Rowan. Rowan slipped her arm around her shoulders. She felt safe. She felt like her world had finally slid into place and everything was as it should be.

"There's something I have to tell you, Rowan."

Rowan kissed her temple. "What?"

"I know it's really soon. I know I barely know you on an intimate level. I know this is crazy."

Rowan shifted and looked into her eyes. "I love you, Kelly. I'm just crazy about you. I don't want to spend another moment of my life without you by my side."

Kelly felt tears bubble to the surface. Her vision blurred as they ran over. "I love you too, Rowan. With all my heart and soul. That's what I was going to tell you."

Rowan carefully took the coffee cup out of her hand.

God, her eyes are the most beautiful shade of blue. She felt herself loosen inside as Rowan gently leaned forward and kissed her. In that one moment, Kelly knew that Rowan was telling her the truth, that there were no secrets between them, and that they *belonged* together. They had their whole lives ahead of them, and they would spend them together.

"I love you so much," Kelly said, smiling and stroking Rowan's face.

Rowan took a deep, shaky breath. "This is the absolute *best* Saturday morning I've had for a *very* long time." She was silent for a moment. "What happened to us, Kell?"

"I don't know," Kelly said. *Should I ask? Yes. The question's not going to scare her off.* "You're a rich woman, aren't you?"

Rowan looked surprised. "Yes. How did you know?"

"My dream," Kelly said. "There's more. Come."

She slowly disentangled herself from Rowan and stood. She

held out her hand and drew Rowan to her feet. She took Rowan
into the office and opened the filing cabinet and pointed to the
file folder that held Rowan's bank statements.

"There. That's how I know."

Rowan looked stunned. "You can't tell me you've *never* been
in my house."

"No, I haven't. And you *know* that, love."

Rowan blushed. "I don't have an address book loaded with
numbers of women."

Kelly's mind flashed an image of her leafing through a worn
address book and dull pain flowed through her. "I know. *My*
Rowan just isn't like that."

Rowan leant over and moved the mouse on her laptop and
the screen flickered to life. "No electronic address book either."

"And the desktop bitmap is different." Kelly almost shook
with relief.

Rowan sighed. "We didn't have a dream, did we?"

Kelly shook her head. "The more we go on, the less I think
we did."

"What happened to us?"

"No idea." Kelly took Rowan back to the living room.

"I don't think that it was good. In fact, I think it was terrible."
Rowan took a deep breath. "But outside of that, I think you're
the best thing that happened to me."

Kelly smiled and kissed her. "Do you want to try and find out
what happened?"

"That's the real question, isn't it? Do you really want to know?"

"I have to think about it. To be honest, I'm just glad we're
together again."

"So am I." Rowan slipped her arms around Kelly and held
on tight.

Kelly took a deep breath of her wonderfully feminine scent
and smiled, feeling content. *I'm going to ask her to marry me.
It's going to be soon.*

Rowan shifted slightly and looked into her eyes. "About your
living arrangements."

"Ah. Yes. Genevieve." Genevieve felt a million miles and years behind her.

"Do you want to move in with me?" Rowan bit her lip and looked uncertain.

Kelly smiled. "I'd love to. Although, I have to warn you, I'm grumpy in the mornings before coffee."

"I like to work out first thing in the morning."

"I'm a good cook."

"And I'm neat."

"I love gardening."

"I like lawn mowing."

"I want a dog."

"So do I."

Kelly smiled and kissed Rowan. "We only have one problem and it's that we work together."

"It doesn't have to be that way. I got a job offer with Gadgets Inc. I was tossing up taking it." Rowan colored. "I was hesitating because it would have meant that I may not ever seen you again."

"I wouldn't have just let you walk out of my life. That would have killed me. I wasn't in love with Genevieve. I wanted my freedom. I would have come for you."

"I mean that much to you?"

"That much and more. I'm not sure I'm ever going to be able to express to you how much." She gazed at Rowan. "You know, you should say no to Gadgets. Stay. I'll find another job."

Rowan shook her head. "No, I *already* have a new job. Pay's better and there's room to move up. If I go, you'll probably move into my spot."

"How do you know?"

"John's not senior enough and Geoff is an idiot. You're a shoo-in for the position."

"I'm glad you have that much confidence in my abilities."

"I always did and I'm sorry for not being more direct if you ever had doubts."

"Don't you lose all the stock you have in Octahedron if you go?"

"It doesn't matter." Rowan smiled. "First, most of my money

comes from outside Octahedron. Second, I've been building a nest egg forever. Third, I own this house outright. I always wanted to have fun as well as work. I wanted it not to matter if I was out of a job for a while. So I've geared most of my finances with that in mind."

"You know I'm not just with you for your money, right?"

"It's our money, and yes. I know. I can see it in your eyes. You love me."

"Glad you noticed."

"When do you want to get your stuff?"

"Any time you're ready. It feels great to be with you again."

"Again? Yes. Yes, it does."

Kelly cupped her face. "You asked me if I wanted to know what happened to us. I think we both know that what we went through was no dream. I'm half inclined to ask you to find the place we dreamt about. See if we can find out what happened there. But there's another equally large part that's saying we should let the past be the past. We move forward together as a couple from here."

Rowan was silent for a moment. "You mean let sleeping dogs lie?"

Kelly nodded. "What happened to us was real and I don't want to go through it again. It was a nightmare. I felt like we were together and I was so afraid of losing you. I think at one point I did. I can't do it again. Once was enough."

"I agree with you. Curiosity dictates we find out what it was so we don't accidentally do it again."

"And commonsense dictates that if we go back to that town we stand a good chance of it happening again."

Rowan sighed. "You're right." She smiled. "It's funny, you know. I feel the same about this as I did about carrying you across the threshold. It feels like I have a chance to do things differently and I'm going to. I'm making a conscious decision now to let this go. Leave it in the past. Let it be a bad dream. I don't want to lose you either. It'd kill me."

Kelly kissed her. "Then let's go and get my clothes and

be about the business of living." She glanced out of the bay windows. Sun streamed into them and the sky above was a brilliant blue. "It's a beautiful day, you—*we*—live close to the beach and we have the *entire weekend* ahead of us. This is just *magic*."

Rowan smiled and pulled her in close. "There's so much I want to do with you. I know we don't have to do everything in two days, but I want the chance to enjoy some *us* time at our leisure."

"I'm there. I'll *never* turn that down."

EPILOGUE

"I DON'T KNOW what kind of show you think you're running down there, but this is unacceptable."

Rowan stared at her desk phone as though it'd turned into a snake. The feeling of déjà vu was almost overwhelming.

"I apologize," she said smoothly. "I'm not up to speed with your issue. Could you please tell me what the problem is?"

That seemed to upset the man on the other end of the phone. "That's what I thought. Completely unprofessional. Do any of you have any clue what you're doing?"

"Again, Mr. Crossland, I'd like to help you but you have to tell me what's happened."

"Glen Adams is what's happened," Crossland snarled. "He's unprofessional and completely incompetent."

Rowan's eyebrows shot skyward. "*Glen*?"

"Yes. Glen Adams. He comes up here, starts acting like a madman, insults my network manager, runs out of the building and hasn't been back. You're supposed to be the market leader for monitoring software. What kind of joke is this? I expect someone to be at site tomorrow or we're not paying for any of this and we're withdrawing from the contract. Your stockholders aren't going to like any of that once it becomes public knowledge, and it will. *Quickly*."

Oh, hell. David's going to be very *pissed.* Rowan brought up an instant messaging session and eyed her list of contacts. Kelly showed as available. She gave brief grin.

Kelly, you have a minute? I need to see you in my office right now.

"I don't know what's happened," Rowan said. "Let me see what I can do for you."

On my way, replied Kelly.

Crossland was silent a moment. "You'd better sort something out. We paid good money for your solution and we want it in and running before the end of the week."

"I'll call you back in half an hour." Rowan hung up before he could protest.

Kelly appeared in the doorway and Rowan felt herself loosen inside.

"Don't look at me like that," Kelly said breathlessly. "Or you're going to find me under your desk in about five seconds."

"Not that I wouldn't like that," Rowan said. "Very much so, in fact. But yes, you're right. We should both . . . focus . . ." She shook her head. "God, you're so *distracting*."

Kelly looked down at her blouse. "My eyes aren't down there, love. We both have to be professional." She sat down on the other side of Rowan's desk. "Now, boss. What seems to be the problem?"

Rowan shook her head to clear it. "Have you heard from Glen?"

"Yesterday at lunch. Reception in the computer room is horrible so he said he was having trouble checking in. He also said he'd call after he left site. He *did* call while I was on my way home."

Oh, no. Rowan began to feel a nameless dread. "Is he still there? At site?"

"At site? Of course. Well, I presume so."

"We need to know for sure."

Kelly looked at her curiously. "Why? What's the problem?"

"I just go off the phone with a very angry Ryan Crossland. From DoD in Settler's Creek. Apparently Glen was rude, nasty, and incompetent. And he didn't show up to site today."

Kelly stared at her. "*Glen? Are you kidding* me?"

"No." Rowan sighed. "This deal is a lot of money for us. Can we get Glen on the phone?"

Kelly nodded. She gestured toward the phone. "Do you mind?"

Rowan nodded. She had a sick feeling of dread. Kelly looked pale. She dialed Glen's cell number with a shaking hand.

He picked up after a couple of rings.

"Hi, Rowan," Glenn said.

"It's me, Glen," Kelly said. "Are you all right? You're at site, right?"

"Ah, of course I am," Glen said carefully. "What? Did you think I'd take off for no reason?"

"No, of course not," Rowan said quickly. She exchanged a glance with Kelly. She was shaking.

"Rowan just got a call from Ryan. He said you went nuts at site yesterday and you didn't show today."

"Um, I'm here?" Glen said cautiously. "I don't know what he means about me from yesterday. I've been on my best behavior. I'm in Victor's office. We went down to the computer room once yesterday to change out the network card on the server. Other than that I've been well in cell phone reception, just like you asked, Kelly."

Kelly smiled automatically. It didn't touch her eyes. "Good. Thanks, Glen."

"Huh?" Glen said. His voice was muffled. He said something else. Pause. Another rapid spurt of words. "Boss, you there?" he asked clearly. "Victor's just gone to find Ryan. Try and sort this mess out."

"Thanks, Glen," Kelly said. She looked relieved.

"I don't like the computer room, boss."

Kelly's eyebrows shot skyward. "What gives, Glen?"

"It's dark and creepy. I know that sounds weird coming from a grown man but there it is."

"Can you avoid going down there?"

"I'm going to, come hell or high water. Also, boss, is it okay by you if I wrap this up by tomorrow?"

Rowan and Kelly exchanged a glance. Rowan nodded.

"Sure, Glen. Wrap it up and get out of there. We'll refund the extra money they spent for the rest of the week."

"Thanks, boss." Glen gave a gusty sigh of relief. "I'd better go. We're running a little behind because of the network issues yesterday, but I think we can catch up."

"Excellent. Call me at the end of today."

Rowan hung up. She looked at Kelly. "Are you all right?"

"I just want to crawl into your lap," Kelly said. "Does that count as all right?"

Rowan smiled. "I have an odd feeling."

"Like we just dodged a bullet?"

Yes. That. Exactly *like that.* She nodded.

"Yeah," Kelly said, sighing.

Rowan got up, closed her office door, and drew the blinds so they had privacy. She pulled Kelly to her feet and put her arms around her, squeezing tight. She leant down and kissed Kelly, a gentle, loving kiss.

"I feel better now," Kelly whispered when they broke.

Rowan smiled. "I'm glad. I'm relieved." *I feel like whatever it was that happened to us can go away now. I feel like I've been given permission to let go.*

"You want me to wait with you while you call Ryan back?"

"You don't have to. But I wouldn't mind if you did," Rowan said. "I just . . . just . . ."

"I know," Kelly said. "I need to be with you right now too."

Rowan slowly nodded and dialed Ryan Crossland's number.

After five rings he picked up. "Yes? Where's Adams?"

"In Victor's office. He wasn't aware you needed him."

"One moment, please."

Hold music came out of the speaker and Rowan winced. After a moment, the hold music stopped.

"Rowan?"

"Yes, I'm here."

The line was silent for a moment. Ryan cleared his throat. "I apologize for the confusion, Rowan. I spoke too quickly. Victor just came and saw me and told me that Adams was with him."

"That's quite all right. I'm happy to help."

"Thank you."

"You have a good day, Ryan."

"I will. You too."

They hung up.

Rowan looked at Kelly. "It's over. I don't know what happened, but . . . it's over."

Kelly nodded. "Now we can get on with the business of living."

Rowan nodded as Kelly stood. She admired Kelly's form as she stepped to the door. She paused with her hand on the door knob and turned back to Rowan.

"You doing anything for lunch, love?"

Rowan shook her head. "I'm free."

"You want to go to lunch?"

"You're on."

"I'll come and collect you at twelve."

"I'll be waiting for you."

Kelly left.

Rowan turned and looked out of her office window, feeling a sense of hope and normalcy that she hadn't felt for some time.

She watched the boats in Sydney Harbor. It felt like an enormous weight had been lifted from her shoulders. She thought about Kelly and felt her spirits lift. *I've got two hours until lunch.*

Her e-mail dinged and she turned to read it, feeling free for the first time in what felt like forever.

Jordan Falconer was born in Sydney, Australia, and from a very young age had an interest in ghoulies, ghosties and long legged beasties and all things that go bump in the night. After surviving Catholic school (twice!) she graduated from Sydney University with an honors degree in Psychology. She currently resides in California with her other half and two small, demanding dogs.